The
Dead Presidents Club

The Dead Presidents Club

❖

Tom Paine's "Common Sense" for the 21st Century

A Novel

Harris I. Baseman

iUniverse, Inc.
New York Bloomington Shanghai

The Dead Presidents Club
Tom Paine's "Common Sense" for the 21st Century

iUniverse books may be ordered through booksellers or by contacting:

iUniverse
1663 Liberty Drive
Bloomington, IN 47403
www.iuniverse.com
1-800-Authors (1-800-288-4677)

Because of the dynamic nature of the Internet, any Web addresses or links contained in this book may have changed since publication and may no longer be valid.

ISBN: 978-0-595-51789-3 (pbk)
ISBN: 978-0-595-62033-3 (ebk)

Printed in the United States of America

Preface

I was operated on at the Beth Israel-Deaconess Hospital in Boston, Massachusetts on September 23, 2006. Eighteen days later, I was released from the hospital, and I returned home. For many of those eighteen days, I was not fully aware of what was going on or what I did. Friends and family claim that I engaged in bizarre telephonic activities. I will neither admit nor deny those allegations and I will speak no further about them, but sometime during my stay in the hospital, the idea for this book entered my head and it would not go away.

At the time of my hospitalization, I was working on my third novel, *Turn-coats*. Once I began to feel better, I resumed working on my novel and managed to put aside the idea of writing this book. It reappeared from time to time, but I resisted the urge to work on it. After *Turncoats* was published in November, 2007, my need to write this book re-surfaced. I wrote a dozen pages and stopped. I felt inadequate to the task. I asked a few friends who had read and were entertained by my previous novels to read the pages. I told them I thought it was a great idea for a book, but that someone else ought to write it, someone who was a real historian, someone who had spent a lifetime studying the lives of the presidents of the United States, perhaps someone like Doris Kearns Goodwin. I hope the readers of this book do not decide that my first inclination was right.

In any event, the feedback I got was that I had to finish the book. A college professor friend advised me that academics would be too involved in every nuance of the lives of the presidents and that they would probably not be willing to speculate about today's issues from the point of view of those deceased presidents. When I was nearer to completion of this book, I again furnished pages to friends and critics and again renewed my concern about who should write this kind of book. I was told that I had acquired more than enough knowledge of the presidents to write this book and that I had to finish it and publish it. No one ever told me that about any of my three prior novels. I confess I was not used to the enthusiastic comments I received, especially from readers who told me that they rarely read fiction.

I may well have made mistakes and taken liberties with the political and philosophical positions of some of the presidents. If so, it was not intended. I tried to get it right. My goal however was not to guarantee that any particular president of the United States would have done or said any particular thing concerning today's issues, but rather to present what I think they would have said, based on my knowledge of them. My primary goal was to stimulate the reader to review the issues of the day from a different perspective. If I succeed in doing that, this exercise will have been worthwhile.

Readers of the manuscript have been intrigued with what I wrote about thorium. I researched thorium as best I could. It is perhaps unusual for me, but I again experienced a lack of self-confidence concerning my research into thorium. I recognized that acting as a lawyer for forty years before retiring from that profession and then becoming a fiction writer in no way had prepared me to understand and have confidence in my scientific researches. I needed an expert. Who could be better than a Harvard Physics professor? Only two Harvard Physics Professors. Fortunately I knew two. I want to thank retired Harvard Professor Jack Shapiro for confirming my researched conclusion that nuclear energy provides the best possible way to alleviate the energy problem under currently available technologies. I also want to thank Harvard Professor Mara Prentiss for taking the time to review my thoughts and confirm as accurate my reasons for concluding that thorium is a superior nuclear fuel. Whatever I said about thorium that may be wrong is my error and not that of Professor Prentiss and whatever I said about nuclear energy that may be wrong is my error, and not Professor Shapiro's.

I have included at the end of this book a copy of the US Constitution and a compilation of excerpts from Washington's Farewell Address, John F Kennedy's Inaugural speech and his "Man on the Moon" speech and from Martin Luther King's "I have a Dream" speech as a handy way for readers to review them, if they are so inclined. They are a small portion of the materials I examined during the writing of this book.

For readers who want to know more about thorium as an energy source, I would recommend that they go to *thoriumenergy.blogspot.com/2007/04/overturning-california-reactor-ban.html*. I would especially recommend the April 5 and 6, 2007 postings.

If you want to tell me how much you enjoyed the *The Dead Presidents Club* or that you hated it and me, you may do so by e-mail to The DPCLUB@aol.com.

Harris I. Baseman

Acknowledgement

I want to acknowledge the special encouragement to write and complete this book that I received from long time friend, John M. Peckham III, the author of A Master Guide to Income Property Brokerage, now in its 4th Edition. I also want to thank my wife, Peggy and my daughter, Elise Chadwick and her husband, Michael for their editorial comments. They were beyond helpful and made this book more readable and, I hope, more likable.

1

I looked at my watch. Damn! A few minutes from now, I'll be interviewing a former president of the United States and I'm totally unprepared. Unprepared! That doesn't even begin to describe it. I don't even know which president. Wait a minute. Let me think. Who can it be? Carter, Bush, Clinton. Who else is still around? How did this happen? Who arranged this interview? I'm drawing a complete blank.

The last thing I clearly remember, I was driving down the Mass. Turnpike headed home after my regular shift on the eleven P.M. Eyewitness News. Suddenly, I was staring into this bright light, probably some moron with his high beams on. I remember that the light got brighter and brighter until I was almost blinded. That was it. And here I am now, sitting on a sun-shaded patio overlooking the eighteenth green of the most beautiful golf course I'd ever seen, and that wasn't even the biggest puzzle. How did I get here? I don't remember a thing. Am I having some kind of senior moment? I felt a lump in my pocket where I usually kept a slim pad with notes and reminders. Maybe Ellie from the station prepared something for me and I forgot about it. I pulled the lump out of my pocket—nothing. No notes, no reminders, only a packet of one dollar bills. I looked at that familiar face a moment and returned George Washington to my pocket. I then glanced at the second hand on my wristwatch. It was only a few ticks before noon. I took a deep breath and decided to just suck it up and do it. I didn't have time to think about being unprepared. I knew a fair amount about Carter, Clinton and Bush. My mystery guest would appear soon enough and I'll see who it is that I have to interview. I'll just have to do the best I can.

A moment later, I saw a tall man at the far end of the room. As he approached, I noticed he wore strange looking clothes, even for a golf club, black knickers, white stockings and a white, long sleeved, puffy shirt under a black jacket. And the shoes, what's with the shoes? They were like pirate shoes, big, black things with silver buckles. I stared at him. Who is it? It wasn't Carter. It wasn't Bush, and it wasn't Clinton. I stared at him again. He did look familiar, but why the funny clothes? I stood to greet him and wracked my brain trying to recall exactly who he was and what I knew about him, but again, nothing came to my mind.

Then, it came to me. It couldn't be, but his was the face I had just looked at on the one dollar bill.

The man smiled as he extended his hand. We shook hands and somehow, the touch of his hand dispelled some of the unease I was feeling. He motioned for me to sit down and then did so himself, facing me, with his back to the eighteenth green. Although his face was the one I saw on the one dollar bill, he looked somehow different. I stared at him. Yes, it's the same face, but the hair is different, a little shorter than on the Stuart painting. How can this be? Should I say something about his resemblance to George Washington and ask him who he was? I don't know why, but I somehow knew I shouldn't do that.

I remembered that I had always understood that President Washington rarely smiled because he had bad teeth, wooden teeth, or maybe bone, I didn't remember which, but it seemed to me that this person smiled quite easily. He smiled again, revealing a momentary glimpse of what looked like almost too perfect teeth. He broke the silence. "I'm pleased to meet you."

I nodded at him, but couldn't say anything.

"You've done this more often than I," he said, "and certainly more recently. How would you like to begin?"

Feeling enormously flustered, I decided to go ahead with whatever the joke was and said, "Mr. President, you are President Washington, aren't you?"

"Of course," he replied. "I look a little different, I know, but it's me. You can look at the wad of bills in your pocket again, if you wish."

"No, no," I said, totally embarrassed. Could he have seen me looking at the money in my pocket? I wondered for just a moment if he could actually be President Washington. I wanted to ask him what was going on here. How did I get here? Who arranged this elaborate hoax and why?

Before I could say anything, he smiled kindly at me and said, "I know you're confused. I assure you, it's really me, George Washington, the first president of the United States of America."

Suddenly, I knew to the very core of my being, it was true. That person in front of me is George Washington. I wanted to kneel before him like he was royalty or kiss his ring or do something to show how overwhelmed I was, but instead, I said, "I want you to know how deeply honored I am that you have chosen to grant me this interview." I didn't know what to say next and blurted out, "Before we do anything else, I have to ask, is this to be off the record, background, or can I quote you?" As the words came out of my mouth, I thought to myself, how could I say something so inane and so stupid?

The president smiled a beatific smile, flashing those perfect white teeth at me, and as he did, the thought flashed through my mind that those rumors of bad teeth had to be nonsense. I wondered if the other stories I had heard about him were also fiction. The president turned serious and said, "Definitely on the record. I discussed this with my fellow club members and we decided that there were to be no subjects that were off-limits, except purely personal matters." He paused a moment. I wanted to ask him who his fellow club members were, but before I could formulate a question, he continued, "I don't want to waste time with extraneous issues. Questions about the personal lives of any of us are unacceptable. For example, I don't want questions about my teeth. I know you wondered about them, most people do. I know you also wonder where you are. I decided I would tell you that." He continued. "You are at the Dead Presidents Club. For some of us, this is a golf course, for others a beach, or a farmhouse, or sometimes a library or a ski slope or a forest. It is what we make of it. That is something the people of your time could strive to do, to make of your time as much as you can, to make your life and that of those who follow as rewarding as possible. For these interviews, I chose this setting for the Dead Presidents Club and made it a golf course because I knew of your love for the game." He took a sip from the cup of tea that somehow had appeared in front of him before continuing. "In conducting these interviews, I want you to be as comfortable as possible in a kind of a setting with which you are familiar. Now, we will speak of those matters no further. Those things are unimportant and detract from the serious issues we are going to talk about. I'm sure you understand."

I nodded that I did and again wondered if President Washington had mind-reading abilities.

The president remained serious and unsmiling as he continued. "What you will hear is on the record, definitely, for the record. That's why we're having this meeting." Washington nodded. "It's been a very long time since I served my country, but I want you to know that my love for this nation and my concern for its well-being and its people remain undiminished by time.

"Think back with me a moment to our beginnings, to the period where, as a colony, we suffered without the freedom and ability to act for ourselves in our own best interest, and to our first failed effort after we achieved independence. We were a weak and puny association of states experimenting in self-government with no success until we adopted the Constitution. It is under that Constitution and that form of self government that we have flourished, flourished to a point where the United States has become the most powerful nation on earth and uniquely so. Consider that contrary to most other powerful nations in the history of the world, we do not seek to subjugate others with our military might for our own pecuniary gain. Instead," Washington said with a smile and twinkle in his eyes, "we try to bring liberty and freedom to everyone, sometimes whether they want it or not." The president's mood changed and he frowned for a moment. "Despite all our good intentions, we have become the most misunderstood nation in the entire history of this planet." Washington shook his head sadly. "Most recently, many things have occurred that worry me and my associates about your future, and indeed, the future of all the inhabitants of this planet."

"Is that why you decided to grant me this interview?"

"Yes it is. We're all retired now so we spend a lot of time watching what goes on in our country and the rest of the world. Golf, tennis and other sporting activities—those things are diversions for us, not a way of life." The president smiled. "Perhaps that's because no one plays well enough to take the games too seriously." Washington paused a moment. "Even those of us who enjoy burying themselves in books or the great outdoors take great interest in the future of mankind." Serious again, he continued, "We all have the time to consider and reflect on current events in your time. We get together almost every afternoon to discuss what's going on and talk about it. We decided that someone had to step up to right the ship of state and steer it out of the shoals onto a safer course. Unfortunately, we don't see any current political leader here or elsewhere who we believe can do that. I was selected by the members of the club to try and express our views, and hopefully, help the nation correct its course. We decided to invite you to talk with us, with the hope that these interviews might help our countrymen deal with the problems of today."

Before I could protest and say I doubted I was the right person to deliver that message, President Washington continued, "Some of us wanted to write a series of essays, something like the Federalist Papers, but it seems that the people of your time prefer to watch TV and listen to the radio rather than read the printed word. That's why we decided on this kind of interview format where you ask questions and we answer them."

I felt momentarily flustered and unsure. What should I ask him about? Before I could say anything, the president said, "Don't worry, you'll ask good questions."

I took a deep breath and began. "Tell me sir, do you think it's possible to 'right the ship of state and steer it onto a safer course?' I think that's what you described it as."

"Certainly, we've had much bigger problems than what we are now experiencing. When we began this nation, we were a group of insignificant, former British colonies with diverse interests, separated in so many ways. We have been tested many times since the Revolution. Very early on in 1812 in the second war with Great Britain, again during the War Between the States and in World War I and II. The 'Cold War' with Communism had its wars of containment in Korea and Viet Nam, and fortunately ended without the nuclear confrontation that had been threatened, but most of those wars presented problems, very much like those of today. We overcame those prior difficulties and we can defeat the current threat."

"What do you see as the current threat, Mr. President?"

"It's the threat posed by religious fanatics who embrace a culture of violence and want to deprive us of our freedom, our liberty and of our very survival."

"You mean the Muslim religion?"

"No, from fanatics who claim that religion. In the past, there were other religions that produced fanatics that threatened to kill and destroy in the name of their religion. At one time, Christianity produced such fanatics. At this time, the threat comes from fanatics within Islam who want to impose their interpretation of the teachings of that religion on everyone else. Consider, that at its height in the thirteenth and early fourteenth centuries, it was a tolerant religion and culture that embraced Jews and Christians and was the most advanced civilization of its day. Visit some of the buildings in Spain and Istanbul. They are incredible. Later, its leaders became intolerant of any deviation from the most rigid interpretation of its rules, including deviation by other Muslims, and it punished those deviations with floggings, mutilations and beheadings. That civilization then declined, but the repressive fanaticism continued and has grown. Here, we call them Islamic Fascists and the threat they make is really nothing new."

I nodded in agreement although I had some reservation and said, "Many of my contemporaries would agree with you, but they see it as a unique problem, one against a religious philosophy rather than as a dispute with any particular government. That's why we have that mess in Iraq with an unpopular war that almost no one wants to see us continue. They say it's not like other wars we fought and no one seems to know what we should do."

Washington smiled sadly. "I must disagree with that. It's very much like other wars we fought. Think about it. Our Revolutionary War was to resist the idea of the divine right of kings and to obtain liberty and freedom for the American people. The War Between the States was initially to preserve the union of states we established and then ultimately, to secure those very same rights for which we fought, for people deprived of those rights for racial reasons. Without that union, we would have become a group of diverse states with separate interests, quarrelling among ourselves and with the rest of the world. It took great skill and leadership by President Lincoln to preserve the nation and remove a compromise on slavery that many of us opposed, but which was necessary for our founding. The problems from that original compromise continue to some extent even today." Washington sipped his tea for a moment before continuing. "World War II and the Cold War were both fought to preserve freedom and liberty against totalitarian forms of government, fascism and communism. There, foreign powers wanted to impose their systems on the rest of us. The most significant current threat is very similar to those that I've just described. A rigid Muslim theocracy wishes to impose its rule over the rest of the world and deprive you of your liberty and freedom and of your very lives."

I thought that perhaps the president didn't see the difference I saw and said, "Excuse me sir, but that still seems to me to be a war against a religion, a religion that millions of people throughout the world embrace in a number of countries. That seems different from the conflicts you mentioned which were fought against specific governments."

The president had listened intently. He nodded at me and said, "It is a war against a theocracy that combines religion with government. We in the United States separated church and state. That was one of our most important contributions to the world. The present enemy rejects that notion and insists that government and religion be in the hands of the same ruling parties. It insists that its interpretation of religious laws takes precedence over all other laws. When the church and state combine, the result is often a war against other states and religions, against anyone who will not accept their domination." Washington frowned. "Religious wars pitting one religion against another are nothing new. They go back to biblical days. That's why we separated the state and religion. The current threat the world has to deal with is really nothing new. Our Constitution guarantees freedom of religion and prohibits the establishment of any religion. Where that is not the case and they are combined, a war against a government becomes a war against the religion which that government supports. The United States should not be reluctant to go to war against a theocracy that is dedicated to its destruction or to any adherents to that theocracy wherever they may be. It is not reasonable to refuse to answer a threat to your survival because the civil side of the theocracy doesn't openly embrace the murderous aims of its clergy." The president paused a moment. "As a matter of fact, the United States had to deal with attacks against it and its citizens by a Muslim theocracy very early in our history."

I thought to myself that I was better informed than the average person and if I didn't understand what the president was saying, most people wouldn't. Puzzled and somewhat embarrassed, I asked, "Excuse me, sir, but I'm afraid I don't remember my American history well enough to know what you're referring to."

"Not many people do," the president replied with a smile intended to put me at ease. "That problem existed while I was president and I didn't do much about it because I had so many other things to take care of." With a twinkle in his eyes, the president continued, "I know just the man to tell you about it."

As if by magic, a slim, distinguished looking man approached our table. He was dressed in much the same fashion as President Washington. He said, "Good afternoon, George." Looking at me, he continued, "He must be the journalist we were expecting."

"He is," the president said. Turning to me, he said, "I'd like you to meet my friend, Tom Jefferson. He can tell you what he did about the attacks on American interests by Muslims when he was president."

2

Jefferson shook my hand, and then sat down beside President Washington. I was still in a state of shock from meeting President Washington, and now here was Thomas Jefferson, the third president of the United States. I stared at Jefferson and then Washington. I mentally compared Jefferson's face with the one I saw on the infrequent two dollar bills that I remembered seeing and with the portrait that adorned the many, many nickels that had passed through my fingers. My God, I thought, he's the man that wrote the Declaration of Independence. Sensing my inability to do more than just stare at Jefferson, President Washington said, "Thomas, tell our guest about the little war we fought while you were president."

Jefferson nodded and then said, "It was the war with the Barbary Coast pirates that George refers to as 'the little war'. If you remember your history, there were Muslim states that used to terrorize shipping in the Mediterranean and the Atlantic during our colonial days and for many years thereafter. For example, two of our ships, one from Boston and one from Philadelphia were seized in 1784." Jefferson smiled and nodded in Washington's direction as he said, "The problem got worse while George was president, and I wanted to do something about it, but nobody would listen to me."

Jefferson smiled almost indulgently at President Washington and then turned back towards me. "In all fairness to George, the problems pre-dated his taking office on April 30, 1789." Jefferson paused a moment, seeming to be far off in some other dimension. He continued, "That was the glorious day on which our nation really began. It was before then," Jefferson stopped himself a moment and then continued. "It was in 1786 during the confederacy. I was ambassador to France and John Adams was ambassador to Britain. We met in London with Sidi Haji Abdul Rahman Adja, who was the ambassador to Britain from Tripoli. As I informed the Continental Congress, I asked him why, without provocation of any kind, his people attacked our ships at sea. He told me that it was founded on the Laws of their Prophet; that it was written in the Koran that all who do not acknowledge their authority are sinners and that it was the right and duty of all Muslims to make war upon them, wherever they may be, and make slaves of all their prisoners." Jefferson frowned and shook his head. "Adja went on to tell us that any Muslim slain in battle would surely go to Paradise.

"Even though I opposed it, we decided to go along with the French and British and participated in a program of appeasement. I didn't believe in appeasement then and still don't. The British and French and other Europeans had a predisposition towards appeasement, a very serious failing it seems to me, and it also seems to me that they still have it. World War II could have been so easily prevented if the Europeans had any courage, but they didn't and millions died. Never would have happened if I were around. All you had to do was read Hitler's book, *Mein Kampf,* to know what he intended to do. It was all there in black and white."

Washington smiled good naturedly at Jefferson. "Tom we all know how smart and principled you are." Turning towards me he said by way of explanation, "I'm sure you remember Jack Kennedy's famous quip. One time after he had a large group of brilliant people at a White House dinner he said that there hadn't been that much brainpower at a White House dinner since the last time Tom Jefferson dined there alone. That remark has made Tom even more insufferable." Still smiling at Jefferson, Washington said, "But, let's see if we can stick to the point, Thomas. Tell our guest what was going on and what you did."

"Insufferable indeed," Jefferson said with a smile. "I'll let that pass for now." Turning towards me, Jefferson said, "All appeasement really did was confirm to the rulers of those pirates that we, along with the Europeans, were only paper tigers." Jefferson waggled a finger at President Washington and me as he said, "Sound familiar?" Without waiting for an answer, Jefferson continued, "I read the Muslim holy book, the Koran, so I could better understand the nature of that enemy. They say that paying tribute is required by their holy book to avoid the requirement of conversion to their religion or death. After I read it, I concluded that trying to reason with them was stupid, as it would be with any religious zealot, and was a waste of time. It was clear that their aim was to rule all the rest of us and impose their religion on everyone who wouldn't pay tribute to them. Modesty prevents me from saying much more although I do love to hear George admit that I was right. By the way, did you know that I donated my copy of the Koran to the library of Congress and that very Koran was used on January 4, 2007 to swear in Congressman Keith Ellison who is a Muslim?"

Washington interrupted. "When Tom became president, he finally had his way. He said, 'millions for defense but not one cent for tribute' and went to war against the Barbary States. Tom always had a way with words. Anyway, Thomas sent the navy to bombard their ports and then sent the Marines in to take Tripoli. The rulers of those Muslim states then agreed to cease and desist from any further attacks upon us." The president smiled and said, "In case you've forgotten, the Marine's Hymn commemorates that victory. I won't try to sing it for you but the words are as I remember them, *'From the halls of Montezuma to the shores of Tripoli, we will fight our country's battles on the land as on the sea.'* You remember that now, don't you?"

I nodded that I did. "That's very interesting, but I'm sure you agree that things are quite different now."

"I agree," Washington said. "The threat now isn't to our commercial interests and the men who traverse the seas, but to our whole way of life and to our very existence. The religious fanatics among the Muslim population of today have stolen the religion from the moderates and are dedicated to killing each and every one of us. You can read it for yourself in the writings of Osama Bin Laden, just as you could have read about the goals of the Nazis in Hitler's *Mein Kampf* and of the Communists in the writings of Karl Marx. Tom is very right about that. Just as the many peaceful Germans were no deterrent to the Nazis and the peace-loving Russians were no deterrent to the Soviets, the many peaceful Muslims are no deterrent to the Islamic Fascists."

I nodded in agreement and said, "You are undoubtedly right, sir, but I meant that the problems we now have can't be solved with a bombardment of some ports and a few detachments of Marines."

Washington nodded at me. "Exactly so. Modern times and problems require modern solutions. Here's another member of our club with views on the subject."

Suddenly, the chair previously occupied by Thomas Jefferson was vacant and I saw a short man wearing a double-breasted, business suit and eyeglasses approaching. His face wasn't on any money. I knew that face, but I was having trouble putting a name to the face until Washington rose to welcome him and said, "I'd like you to meet the thirty-third President of the United States, Harry S. Truman. He comes from a state that wasn't even part of the country when I was president."

Truman stood ramrod straight as he shook my hand. He then polished his eyeglasses, replaced them and finally sat in the chair on which Jefferson had been seated. "How do you do young fellow," he said with a kind of mid-western twang. "I saw Tom leaving, so you must have heard about how he sent some frigates and a few detachments of Marines to stop the attacks by the Barbary Coast Muslims."

Washington said, "Yes, and," pointing at me, he continued, "our young visitor thinks Tom's solution couldn't work in these times."

Truman said, "I agree and so does Tom. Current technology is such that you might have to use nuclear bombs if you were to presently follow Tom's views. Conventional weapons don't seem to end the problem."

"Is that what you would do?" I asked.

Truman sat back a moment and then said, "No president of the United States wants to be the person who authorizes the use of so fearful a weapon and then becomes responsible for so many deaths. But, when you sit in the oval office, the buck stops there. I bombed Hiroshima and Nagasaki to end World War II and remain convinced that it was the right decision. I know some people criticize me for it, but I was president of the United States, not president of the world, and it was my job to win the war and lose as few of our people as possible. I was convinced that we saved lives, those of our men and, as a matter of fact, many Japanese lives as well by that decision."

"Excuse me, sir, but you didn't use nuclear weapons in the Korean War, how come?" I asked.

Truman frowned. "I was tempted, but that was different. In my judgment, the use of nuclear weapons at that time might have led to an enlargement of the conflict to include China and possibly the Soviet Union and to nuclear retaliation by the Soviets. I decided that it was not in our best interest to run that risk and I saw no danger to the survival of our nation. The current situation may pose a much greater threat, one to our very survival as a free people, like World War II did. If or when it does, I would not hesitate a moment."

Shocked at the possibility, I said, "Do I understand that you would recommend the use of nuclear weapons?"

Truman shook his head. "Not immediately. If I were to become convinced that we had to use nuclear weapons, I would suggest that we first send a strong statement to all Muslim governments and people."

"What kind of statement?" I asked.

"I thought you'd ask me that." Truman polished his eyeglasses with his handkerchief, then pulled a sheet of paper from his inside breast pocket and read from it.

"To the rulers of all Islamic nations and peoples—

Be advised that the United States will not tolerate any further attacks on its peoples or interests anywhere in the world. Any nation or region that is complicit in or gives aid and comfort to anyone attacking us will suffer dire consequences. Those consequences will include nuclear retaliation. So that there will be no mistake about it, if in our judgment, Iran, Iraq or Syria is involved, in an attack upon us, there will be retaliation with a nuclear attack on Tehran, Baghdad or Damascus. The same goes for Pakistan, Afghanistan or the people of any other place who are foolish enough to participate in the killing of our people."

Truman shook his head as he returned the slip of paper to his pocket and said, "I think that's plain enough." He smiled a moment. "LBJ suggested I tell them to kiss their ass goodbye, but that didn't sound very presidential to me." He paused a moment and became serious. "I certainly would hate to be the president who has to decide to push the button. But I believe that if the situation was reversed, and they had nuclear capability, the Islamic Fascists wouldn't hesitate or need the provocation of a prior attack to wipe out New York, Washington or some other American city."

I frowned as I said, "Do I understand that you, President Truman, and that President Jefferson and President Washington are all committed to a proposal that a notice like that you read to us should be issued right now?"

"Perhaps." Truman asked, "Tell me, do you have any doubt that the terrorists in those lands would use that weapon right now if they had it?"

I said, "I really don't know, sir, but are you advocating that the United States use nuclear bombs in Iraq and against countries like Iran and Syria?" Turning to President Washington, I said, "And do you agree with that, sir?"

President Washington didn't answer my question. Instead, he said, "Iraq repeatedly attacked our forces after the 1991 Gulf War. Before that, Iran seized our embassy and held our people hostage and it continues to this day to use its forces to kill our people in Iraq. Syria continues to aid and abet everyone that does attack us. If I were president, it would be hard not to do exactly that. The United States has been repeatedly attacked by Middle East terrorist forces, most dramatically on Sept 11, 2001, and as Harry said, the president's job is to protect the American people and not let our military forces be killed if it could be prevented. I tell you very seriously, that if the survival of this nation were to be threatened by those theocracies and I'm convinced that the threat is imminent, I would not hesitate a moment."

I was surprised even shocked. It seems that Truman and perhaps even Presidents Jefferson and Washington were all in favor of the use of nuclear weapons.

President Washington must have noticed the surprised look on my face as I said, "I can't believe any president could authorize the use of nuclear weapons."

Washington smiled almost grimly at me and then said, "As Harry frequently says, if you can't stand the heat, you ought to get out of the kitchen. A president may be called on to do unpleasant things and has to be prepared to do them."

Truman smiled at me a moment. "I did what I did and I'm here, so that must mean I did the right thing."

With that statement, Truman rose from his chair, he nodded at President Washington and me and he then seemed to vanish before my eyes. I wondered what he meant when he said he was here. What is this place? I wanted to ask President Washington that question, but recalled that those matters were not allowed. Instead I said, "Tell me sir, do you agree with President Truman that we ought to go nuclear?"

Washington smiled at me. "It's time for lunch. We can talk about Truman's opinions later, but you ought to think about it for yourself before we do and if you think appeasement is a solution you ought to listen to President Kennedy first. He has strong views on the subject. He's joining us for lunch. Now, what would you like?"

"What do they have?"

"Everything. Jack's having his usual Friday lunch, New England Fish Chowder and a fish sandwich with a side of baked beans and some fruit. I'm having beef stew and rice pudding. I highly recommend the rice pudding. It's Martha's recipe."

I suddenly felt ravenous. "Could I get some of that fish chowder and I'd love to try that rice pudding, and could I get a cheeseburger and fries, and maybe a Coke?"

"Sure can." Moments later JFK approached our table. He looked very young and boyish compared to Presidents Washington, Jefferson and Truman. He was wearing tan slacks and a navy blue golf shirt. Washington said, "How'd you play today?"

"Don't ask," he replied as he sat down where Thomas Jefferson and then Harry Truman had just been seated. "I used to have a bad back as an excuse, but not anymore. I had a bad day and Ronnie, Ike and Gerry all had splendid rounds. I couldn't make a putt all morning." He grinned at me and then said, "Perhaps I ought to stick to sailing."

President Washington said, "You're spending a lot of time with Republicans lately. It almost seems like you're abandoning the Democrat party."

JFK shook his head almost sorrowfully. "Not so, George. Truth be told, I think they abandoned me. You remember my Inaugural Address where I said ask not what your country should do for you. I meant it. I don't believe in most of those government entitlement programs. I always believed in small government, but enough of that. I'm being rude to your guest." Looking at me, he offered his hand and said, "I'm Jack Kennedy. Nice to meet you. I assume you know that questions about Jackie and Marilyn are off limits."

"Yes."

"Good." We've got a little time before lunch. We ought to get started. Okay with you, George?"

Washington nodded in agreement. "Fine with me."

President Kennedy then turned towards me and said, "Now, what do you want to start with?"

"I guess it's the current world situation, particularly the War against Terror, so-called. I gather from my interviews of Presidents Jefferson and Truman that they're in favor of a nuclear solution to the problem."

President Kennedy frowned. "Perhaps, but they can speak for themselves. What do you want to ask me?"

I wanted to ask him if he, like Jefferson and Truman, was in favor of a nuclear attack but didn't want to make that my first question. Instead I asked, "Are you in favor of sending a warning to the Muslim world of the possible nuclear destruction of Tehran, Baghdad and/or Damascus in the event of another attack on the United States?"

"Not necessarily at this time, but I am convinced that a policy of appeasement should not be tolerated." Kennedy continued, "Many years ago, I said in my Inaugural Address, '… *let every nation know that we shall pay any price, bear any burden, meet any hardship, support any friend, and oppose any foe to assure the survival of liberty*'." He paused a moment and then said, "And whose liberty is more precious than our own? When I said that I believed it was the best course for our country to follow and still do. Now let me say this, so far as appeasement is concerned, I said then that that those who foolishly seek power by riding on the back of the tiger should beware that they not end up inside. I believe that still. I think that many Europeans are beginning to regret their appeasement policies and fear that it's too late for a course correction."

"Then you do believe, like Presidents Jefferson and Truman, that we ought to nuke Iran, Iraq and Syria?" I asked.

JFK smiled and said, "I feel the same way George does about that. Ask him."

I did, but President Washington only stared into space for a moment, and then turned to me and said, "Our lunch is here, we will resume after lunch."

3

During lunch, our conversations were off-the-record, but President Washington said I could repeat what he told me about the club when I asked him if all deceased, former presidents were members of the club.

He replied, "All but two. Calvin Coolidge didn't want to join and Warren G. Harding re-considered before we voted. Some of us were doubtful about Richard Nixon, but not enough to keep him out."

"What do you think about our current, living presidents? Will they all become members?"

President Washington thought a moment and then said, "When his time comes, many of us think Jimmy Carter will be the first president to be denied membership if he seeks admittance."

Surprised, I asked, "Why is that?"

"He had a dismal record as president. He left the economy in shambles and more importantly, his doing nothing about the Iranians making hostages of our embassy people is a root cause of all of the difficulties we have with that part of the world to this day. It was the same kind of weakness Neville Chamberlain exhibited when he dealt with Hitler's seizing Czechoslovakia and it has had the same effect. It's a good thing Tom Jefferson isn't having lunch with us. He thinks Carter is a fool. Then, there are Carter's current close ties, personal and financial, with certain members of the Saudi Royal family that we think are inconsistent with his moral obligations as a past president of the United States. Finally, there are his comments and his conduct concerning the Middle-East. We believe he is just plain wrong and that he is acting in a manner that is contrary to the best interests of the United States. There are a number of us, who agree with John Adams and regard his conduct as bordering on treason."

"Treason? That's pretty strong."

"Yes, it is."

"May I ask if you agree with that?"

"You may not."

I really wanted to know what he thought about Carter, but I knew better than to ask the same question again. "May I ask," I said, "would you, personally, be in favor of his admittance to the club?"

"He's not eligible right now."

"But if he were," I persisted.

Washington remained silent a moment. I was afraid I had angered him. He finally said, "Probably not, but let's move on."

Could I push my luck? I found this fascinating. "What about Bill Clinton and George Bush, the younger?" I asked. "Will they become members of this club when their time comes?"

Almost wearily, but good naturedly, as if resigned to satisfy the need I had to satisfy my curiosity, Washington said, "Neither was a very good president in my opinion, and Clinton's lies to the Congress and the people are an additional problem for him, but I don't think either of them will be denied admission. Now, that's enough of that."

I knew better than to ask him any more on that subject and turned back to my lunch. After we finished eating I returned to the main topic and remarked that I found it difficult to believe that he, along with Presidents Jefferson, Truman and Kennedy were willing to launch what seemed to me to be a nuclear holocaust.

President Washington replied, "You misunderstood Tom, Harry and Jack. None of them advocate an immediate nuclear solution, nor do I; but as Jack would say, make no mistake about it, if we have no alternative, none of us would hesitate." He paused a moment and looked at me with a very worried expression on his face. He continued, "I'm very sorry to say, that the time is fast approaching where we will have no other alternative. Right now, there's still a chance to avoid that kind of drastic solution, but we have to start solving that problem right now."

President Kennedy interjected, saying with that unique speech pattern I found so engaging, "I agree that the window of opportunity for a peaceful solution is closing." Shaking his head slowly from side to side, he continued, "I certainly cannot fathom what the difficulty is with the current leadership group in government. Think back to our early years. Accomplished, successful, brilliant and well off patriots put their lives and fortunes at risk to oppose what was one of the most powerful governments of that age to obtain freedom and liberty for themselves and their heirs. Now, your leaders seem to only think of what they must do to obtain and maintain their personal political power." Obviously upset, President Kennedy said, "It's disgraceful. They should be ashamed."

President Washington looked towards Kennedy and placed a restraining hand on Kennedy's arm. "Easy, Jack, I find them sadly lacking also. That's why we're doing these interviews." Turning to me, Washington said, "We all find it mystifying that the people of your time continue to finance the Islamic Fascists in their war against themselves. You must realize that is precisely what you are doing. If this continues for very much longer, the Islamic Fascists will have the economic power to amass the weapons they need to destroy the United States."

JFK nodded in approval as he said, "Once they do that, there is nothing to prevent them from taking over the rest of the world if we fail to act."

I thought I understood what Washington and Kennedy had just said, but I wasn't completely certain that I did. "Just who does this financing of terrorism?" I asked.

President Washington, looking a little surprised at the question, said, "The people of the United States and of the rest of the industrialized world—you are providing the Islamic Fascists with the money they need to wage war against yourselves. Forgive me if I didn't make that clear."

"I thought that's what you meant," I said, "but this is very important and I want to be sure."

"I agree that it's very important that the issue be completely understood."

I continued, "Then, excuse me, President Washington. Are you talking about our purchasing Middle East oil?"

"Of course, what else could it be?" President Washington frowned. "Sorry, I thought it was obvious. Part of the money you all pay for Mid-East oil ends up in the hands of the Islamic fascists as payments from the oil sheiks to be left alone." Washington paused, reflected a moment, and then continued. "This is not a new problem. You've known for over fifty years that your reliance on fossil fuels for your energy needs presented a problem that had to be solved, and the United States has been unable or unwilling to do anything about it. Right from the beginning, I preached that our country had to become as self-reliant as possible. It galled me when I was president that we had to import so much from Europe. This is much worse. You need to do something and do it now. If you continue to send your wealth to the oil sheiks who fund the terrorists just so they will be temporarily left alone, the only option you will have to preserve your liberty and freedom will be a nuclear one. You see, that don't you?"

I nodded that I did and I really did. I then asked, "Do you think we can end our dependency on Mid-East oil?"

"Of course you can." Turning to JFK, President Washington said, "I always admired Jack's approach to solving a grave crisis. That's the approach the leadership of your time should take. I especially liked how he handled the space race issue with the Soviet Union. Tell him about that, Jack."

JFK nodded and then said, "One of the main issues back in the early 1960's was our failure to keep up with the Soviets in the space race. On May 25, 1961 in a speech before Congress I said: '*we have examined where we are strong and where we are not. Now it is time to take longer strides—time for a great new American enterprise—time for this nation to take a clearly leading role in space achievement, which in many ways may hold the key to our future on Earth*'. That statement is more applicable to our current energy problem today than it was to the Soviet lead in space exploration in 1961."

President Washington smiled warmly at JFK as if he were his favorite son and said, "I am in total agreement. Repeat some more of that speech, Jack. I'm sure you remember it. It's as compelling to the current situation as it was then."

JFK nodded in agreement as he said, "I agree that what I said then is even more applicable to the current energy crisis than it was to the space race of the 1960's." He then shut his eyes and began to recite from memory, '*I believe we possess all the resources and talents necessary. But the facts of the matter are that we have never made the national decisions or marshaled the national resources required for such leadership. We have never specified long-range goals on an urgent time schedule, or managed our resources and our time so as to insure their fulfillment.*' I said in that speech, that '*I believe that this nation should commit itself to achieving the goal, before this decade is out.*'" He opened his eyes again as he said, "I believe we must do no less than that now. Only in that way can we avoid the necessity of killing millions of people to insure our own survival as a free people."

President Washington added, "As I said before, it is absolutely ludicrous that you continue to finance the war against yourselves by purchasing oil from the Middle-East. You need someone to step forward and say as Jack did that we have to do this, and do it now."

Although I had heard many politicians decry our energy dependency over the years, I hadn't heard it put quite that way before. I said. "Energy independence is a worthwhile goal. I've heard that said many times, but nothing seems to happen. If you were one of us in the present day, how would you make it happen?"

President Washington nodded in agreement, accepting the assumption, and then said, "The first thing we need is the national commitment to accomplishing that goal like the commitment we made to the space race in Jack's time. And we need leaders to articulate it and do it. President Roosevelt, FDR, not Teddy, did that with the Manhattan project for the development of the atom bomb. That's the first thing we need."

"What practical things would you do?" I asked. "I've heard it said that increasing per gallon auto mileage requirements might even be enough."

President Washington nodded, "Conservation is a fine start, but it cannot replenish a depleting commodity. For your survival, you must stop your dependency and create alternative fuel supplies."

"What do you suggest?" I asked.

"There are many things." Turning to JFK again, Washington said, "Jack, tell him what you wanted to do with the tides."

JFK nodded. "And I would have done it, if Dallas hadn't happened." JFK took a deep breath and then said, "I wanted to harness the power of the tides. I focused on the Bay of Fundy, which is partly on the coast of Maine. It has enormous tides, close to sixty feet. I'd bet you could still generate enough electricity from that one source alone to fill the need for electric power for the entire East Coast, from Maine to New York. If the Canadian government and their provincial governments of New Brunswick, Nova Scotia and Quebec had cooperated in the project it could have been even bigger and better, but the United States should have proceeded with that project with or without them." JFK paused a moment before continuing. "With the technology of today, you could also anchor devices to the ocean floor and have the tides, coming and going, turn turbines to generate electricity. You could do the same thing in many of your major rivers where the flow from the current would do the same thing."

"What about the environmentalists?" I asked. "They would probably object to that kind of activity in the oceans. Even your brother, Teddy, objected to a wind farm in the ocean near his summer home in Hyannisport."

JFK scowled. "That surprised me. He's my brother, but I don't know what to make of Teddy anymore. I'll talk to him about that some day, but we're not talking about wind farms right now. Hydropower, as I would propose it, wouldn't require building dams that would affect our wildlife, but let me say this about that, I would not tolerate the knee-jerk reaction of the environmentalist lobby to that kind of benign plan. We can't allow a combination of environmental lobbyists and lobbyists for oil, coal and other energy sources to frustrate what should and has to be done for our mutual benefit and for our very survival."

President Washington nodded in approval and added, "That doesn't mean that we abandon conservation or anything else." He smiled as he added, "Ben Franklin must have said, 'Frugality is a virtue'."

Washington looked into my eyes. I felt as if he were looking at my very soul. He said, "I think our views on the possible use of nuclear weapons in the war against terrorism surprised you."

I said nothing, but nodded as non-judgmentally as possible.

Washington continued. "I believe that the development in the United States of a network of nuclear fueled facilities to produce electrical energy, like they did in France and Germany would go a long way towards making the almost unthinkable use of nuclear bombs unnecessary. Personally, I prefer the French model which is many small facilities rather than the German which is for a few massive ones. You should get one hundred percent of your electric power from nuclear energy, as hydropower from the tides and waterfalls and from wind farms, solar energy and bio-mass, but nuclear energy has to be the primary source for inexpensive energy during your time."

"That sounds good," I said, "but there have been many proposals to build nuclear plants. They all fail because, for safety reasons, no one wants them in their backyard, so to speak, and there are, as I understand it, legitimate environmental concerns about waste disposal and using the by-products for bomb making. How do you overcome that?"

"I should have invited Alexander Hamilton to lunch. He would have loved to answer that question."

"Is he a member of the club?" I asked.

"No," President Washington replied, "but he and Ben Franklin are on the permanent guest list." Washington looked at a table in back of me, stood and waved at a man seated there with someone who had a cigar stuck in his mouth and looked like an English bulldog and then signaled him to join us.

As the man approached, I noted that he wore clothing that was very much like the clothes President Washington wore. I looked at his face. His face was the familiar one I saw on the ten dollar bill. It was Alexander Hamilton. "Was that Winston Churchill he's having lunch with?" I asked.

"Yes, they're good friends and Winston is also on the permanent guest list."

After introductions, Hamilton pulled up a chair and said to President Washington, "This must be the journalist."

"Yes, it is. I'd like you to tell him how you think we ought to proceed with locating and building the nuclear energy facilities we need to supply our electricity."

"Very well." Turning to me, Hamilton said, "That's clearly a situation that requires federal preemption. Political hysterics, lobbyists and well-meaning but badly informed environmentalists have combined to frustrate the necessary building of those facilities far too long. For your survival as a free people, you need nuclear power. That is beyond question. Looking at the current situation, I say we should have a federal agency of scientists and engineers determine where those facilities should be, what size they should be and what kind of fuel they should use. Those are not political decisions; they are scientific and economic ones. No community, if asked will want them or the waste they generate so there's no sense to ask them. The French didn't and they built a multiplicity of similarly designed nuclear energy plants in many places with excellent results. The economy and reliability of proceeding with one basic design was good for France and would be good for us."

"Excuse me, Mr. Hamilton, but the melt-down problems and waste disposal issue seem to doom those proposals."

Hamilton frowned at me. "Those difficulties are exaggerated. With today's technology, you can solve those problems, especially if you use thorium as the main fuel in all of those reactors." Hamilton sat back and looked a little less agitated as he continued. "As I understand it, thorium is more plentiful than uranium and it is abundantly available in the United States. It produces far less toxic waste than uranium. It is not susceptible to 'melt-downs' so it's safer to use than uranium; and very importantly, it can not easily be enriched to make bombs. Early on in the development of nuclear energy power plants in the United States, thorium was considered and used. However, a decision was subsequently made to use uranium instead, although, in many respects, it was not as desirable a fuel. I think what caused the decision to use uranium was the ability to easily enrich it into a substance readily useful in bomb making, something which people now consider to be a disadvantage."

"Excuse me sir, but I've never heard of thorium. I don't mean to be insulting, but how do you know about this substance, thorium. Everyone I know says that nuclear reactors are too dangerous to be used in the United States. They point at Chernobyl and at Three Mile Island."

Hamilton frowned and then regained his composure. "Sorry, I have little patience with that kind of uninformed decision-making." He nodded at me a moment and then continued, "I'm not a nuclear scientist, so scientists must ultimately make the decision, but I did consult with Albert Einstein and others before coming to these conclusions. He and the others looked into it. They unanimously confirmed that what I believe to be true and what I just told you about thorium is true. You can look it up yourself and you will quickly learn that using thorium meets all the objections that are usually made to building nuclear powered, electricity-generating power plants. It can be done cheaply, safely and with minimal disposal problems. Nothing is without risk and we should understand that the risk of the loss of our freedom and liberty and of our very lives to Islamic Fascism far exceeds any environmental or other danger from these nuclear plants. I tell you," he said, pounding on the table, "if there were no such thing as thorium or if thorium wasn't feasible, we should proceed with traditional uranium reactors. It has become a question of national survival and our leaders should consult with real scientists on these issues, not political hacks listening to lobbyists for some economic interest." Hamilton paused a moment to compose himself and then continued. "When the scientific community decided to build a facility to experiment with fusion energy rather than fission, they had to locate the laboratory in France, to a new facility in Provence, even though many of the scientists involved were Americans. They had to do so because no American region would allow them to build the facility in their area. That was idiotic because the research facility would not be any danger to anyone." Hamilton forced a smile. "DeGaulle rarely misses a chance to point out the folly of the United States on that one. What you need is a real president and a Congress comprised of real patriots who are more interested in doing what's right and in the best interests of the United States than pandering to lobbyists and parochial concerns. How you put up with the fools who populate the Congress in your time is beyond me."

President Washington glanced momentarily at the table where Churchill was now sitting and chomping on his cigar and then said, "Thanks, Alex, but I think you better go back and sit with Winston before he becomes upset, and convey my apologies to him for dragging away his lunch companion."

As Alexander Hamilton rejoined Churchill, I said to President Washington, "Nuclear plants, tidal energy and the rest would help, but what about our automobiles and trucks and trains and airplanes? And what about our military? Aren't they the main users of oil?"

"Of course they use a lot of oil, but consider this. Cheap electric power would make electric automobiles more feasible. Electric power is available on all of our highways and roads and re-charging facilities can be more ubiquitous than gasoline stations are now. With cheap electric power from the nuclear plants and other renewable sources, the cost per driving mile could be very inexpensive. During the time it takes to build those plants and the distribution system, we could easily run many of our autos, trucks and buses on ethanol. We should have done it twenty-five years ago. Even now, disputes between the corn lobby and the sugar lobby, to say nothing of the oil industry that wants neither of them to succeed, stall all efforts to do anything. It's disgraceful that a country like Brazil could manage to run most of their autos on ethanol made from sugar and we can't. The scientific evidence indicates that sugar is a more efficient, cheaper and better source of ethanol than corn. Corn lobbyists, motivated by greed, try to deny that reality, and politicians who want their support act contrary to the best interests of the nation they work for. When Alexander Hamilton was a boy living in St. Croix, that island was one of the world's major sources of sugar. I think we could grow a lot of sugar in that US possession, in Puerto Rico and in the United States now, and I would certainly prefer buying ethanol from Caribbean, Central American and South American neighbors than importing oil from the Middle-East. Perhaps some of the cocaine growers could be persuaded to grow sugar instead of cocaine with proper incentives." Washington paused a moment. "Perhaps we might talk about the drug problem at a later interview, but that is not the topic for today." Returning to the issue we had been discussing, Washington said, "We have the ability to ultimately solve this problem and alleviate it substantially right now." President Washington regained his usual poised demeanor. "You'll have to excuse me. I do get carried away some times, but that's because I find it so incomprehensibly disgraceful that we have floundered around for so long and at so great a cost." Washington paused a moment. "I don't mean to over simplify it. Perhaps we could some day lessen our oil dependency by using autos fueled by hydrogen cells. It seems to me that the ethanol solution would be more immediate and far less expensive, but the case for hydrogen should be made and listened to and a decision made on what's best for all of us, not for just certain segments of our society. I didn't mean to dwell this long on the subject of alternative fuels, but it is a problem that needs to be immediately addressed. It can't be immediately solved, but a start must be made if we are to avoid the unthinkable."

Washington paused a moment and sighed. "Before lunch you asked if Harry Truman, Tom Jefferson and I thought we ought to use nuclear weapons against Baghdad, Tehran and Damascus. I didn't answer your question then. I think I have now done so, but since it's so important, I'll answer it again." Washington took a deep breath before he continued. "None of us would use a nuclear weapon at this time against anyone. We believe this energy dependency problem has a solution. If solved, the enemy can be vanquished economically, as we did during the Cold War. However, if the country fails to immediately embark on the energy program we discussed and you continue to finance the terrorists' efforts to destroy us, there will come a time when we will have no choice. As I said before, we won the war against communism without a shooting war. It was our economic power and the comparative attractiveness of our system in providing a better way of life for people that eventually prevailed. People behind the Iron Curtain saw the better and more comfortable lives lived by people who enjoyed freedom and liberty, and they wanted that for themselves. Your strongest weapon should be your success. I tell you, the people of your time can win this war against Islamic terrorism that same way, but the United States must act now." Looking very somber, President Washington said, "It can't be said too often.

Failure demands a terrible price. If you continue on the present course, you will have no choice. You will have to go nuclear and indiscriminately kill millions of innocent people or perish yourselves. That will be your only choice."

We both remained silent for a long moment. I felt a chill through my very being. I finally broke the silence and asked, "Why has administration after administration, Democrat and Republican failed to do anything significant about the energy problem and why do you think something meaningful could be done about it now?"

Washington pulled a gold pocket watch from his waistcoat, opened the cover, glanced at it a moment and then rose as he said, "Sorry, but I promised to meet Martha in a few minutes. I'll have to end the interview for the present. Meet me here tomorrow, same time, and I'll answer that question."

I nodded that I would.

4

I wondered how President Washington would explain the failure of our presidents, from FDR to now, to take any real steps to solve the energy problem. I didn't understand why nothing had happened in over fifty years or why he thought it could be solved now. I didn't have to wonder very long, because before I knew it, I was back at the Dead Presidents Club for my second interview, again facing the eighteenth green. Moments later, President Washington was seated in front of me, smiling at me with those perfect teeth.

"Good to see you again," President Washington said. "I'm never sure just how long you will be with us."

I wanted to ask Washington what he meant by that, but before I could, he said, "Did you think about the questions you asked me when we were ending yesterday's interview?"

"Yes."

"Very good. I'm sure you now agree that utilizing a combination of nuclear energy, hydro-electric power, solar energy, wind-power, ethanol and other alternative energy sources could easily end our Mid-East oil addiction."

"I do," I said, "but it seems to me that we have had the ability to pursue most of those solutions for a very long time." I looked at my notes of our previous interview for a moment and then said, "Yesterday I asked you the following question, 'Why has administration after administration, Democrat and Republican failed to do anything significant about the energy problem and why do you think we could solve that problem now?'"

"I remember the question," Washington said, "but I don't recall saying that I thought the problem could be solved immediately. You need to start solving the problem and hope that you will be able to make enough progress fast enough so that you will not face the necessity of invoking a nuclear solution."

"How much time do we have?"

"That's a difficult question. The only answer I can give you is that I just don't know. The United States had the luxury of time to wage an economic war against the Soviets. Both sides had nuclear weapons and neither used them because both feared nuclear annihilation. That stalemate gave the United States decades to demonstrate the superiority of liberty and freedom and win that economic war against the communist ideology. You don't have that kind of time with the Islamic, fascist ideology."

"Why not?" I asked.

President Washington paused a moment. "Do you recall Thomas saying that Ambassador Adja of Tripoli told him that Muslims believe that after death in battle they go straight to Paradise?"

I nodded that I did.

"It's difficult for you and I to understand it, because we value life so much, but the fanatics we are fighting don't fear death as the Soviets did. That is one major difference. Because of that, the United States must also recognize that, if the Islamic fascists had the Soviet arsenal of nuclear weapons, they would use them because they don't fear retaliation and death the way the United States and the Soviet Union did. Remember this, if you remember nothing else. If the United States delays too long and continues to fund the enemy with oil revenues, the enemy will accumulate the financial resources necessary to acquire or develop a nuclear arsenal; and make no mistake about it, the Islamic fascists are willing to use them."

I felt a chill all the way into my bone marrow. "What should we do?"

"There is another statement Adja made to Thomas. Do you also recall that he reported that Adja said that it is the duty of all Muslims to wage war against all who do not acknowledge their authority?"

"I do," I said. As I remembered what Jefferson had said, a feeling of panic began to overtake me. "What can we do to save ourselves? A preemptive attack using nuclear bombs is unthinkable."

"I've told you what the United States must do if it wishes to avoid an ultimate nuclear solution. To extend the period you may have to stall and fight for time by fighting a host of smaller battles while you strive to solve your energy problems. We can speak of that later, if we have time. For now, we should continue our discussion of how we solve our energy dependency problem."

"Fine," I said. "I understand that we must terminate our Mid-East oil dependency and deprive our enemy of the financial resources they need to wage war against us. That brings me back to the still unanswered question. How do we make that happen now, when we have failed so badly for so long?"

"Yes, that is an unfortunate reality, but let's explore it," Washington said. "Why do you think your countrymen have failed so miserably to do anything about their energy dependency problems?"

"I don't know. I suppose there was always something more important. The Korean War, the Viet Nam War, the cold war with the Soviet Union, and there have been domestic issues, like new roads and health care. There must be hundreds, probably thousands of competing things."

President Washington shook his head sadly. "Those are excuses, not reasons. There are other excuses. For a good part of the fifty-year period, the price of oil was low and it provided cheap energy. That too is an excuse and should not have been tolerated. Every responsible person knew that the demand for oil would increase, that the supply is finite, and it should have been expected that the persons controlling the supply would want to maximize their return on their wasting asset. Our leaders knew all that, but did nothing. They fiddled while Rome burned."

I had to agree with President Washington. "Why do the American people put up with that kind of incompetence? Alexander Hamilton asked me that very question when he was here and I had no answer. I'd like to ask you the same question."

Washington thought a moment, and then said, "I have no concise answer, but it seems to me that we Americans have allowed political divisiveness to obscure our national interest. Politics is increasingly partisan and vicious. Well paid and funded lobbyists have access to our leaders and, as the cost of running for office escalated, they have become ever more influential and corrupting. It's difficult, because often, the decisions made seem to make sense, but pursuit of business and political advantage, rather than the national interest, is the motivating factor with most lobbyists and many of our political leaders. It starts with small compromises and grows into bigger and bigger self deceptions."

I wasn't sure what President Washington was referring to and thought about what he said for a moment. "I think I agree with you, but could you give me some examples of just what you mean?"

"Certainly." Washington looked away a moment to gather his thoughts, then turned to me and said, "In many respects, our highway system was in our national interest, but it also suited the business interests of the auto industry, the oil industry, road building contractors and their employees and the Teamsters Union. They combined to get it done and to make sure that automobiles and trucks were to be the main mode for transporting goods and services. At the same time, they also discouraged any expansion or modernization of rail service by not granting subsidies or government aid to the railroads like they did with the trucking industry."

I didn't want to, but I had to interrupt him. I was unaware of any subsidy or government aid to the trucking industry. I said, "Excuse me, Mr. President, but

I'm unaware of the government giving subsidies or aid to the trucking industry. Could you explain what was done and when?"

President Washington nodded. The highways were built with tax money. We consider that aid or a subsidy to the trucking industry. In our time, we were more inclined to have toll roads which were paid for by the users. Whatever you want to call it, no government consideration was given to the building or improvement of the rail roads' 'highways' the rail beds and tracks. The result is our rail service, when compared to that of other western countries, is deplorable. Neglecting rail service had the desired and predictable results. We could have had a few less superhighways and had efficient train service. That would have been better in so many ways. For example, with trains that travel at 200 miles per hour, as they do in Japan and France, suburbs fifty miles from New York City would be only fifteen minutes away. Just think how many automobiles could be taken off the highways with that kind of train service and how much gas could be saved. Another example would be the combination of environmentalists and Middle East and other foreign oil interests that form alliances to prevent oil exploration in other places, like Alaska, or the construction of nuclear energy plants, wind farms, hydro-electric power plants or whatever else may be suggested to help solve the problem. More recently, the corn lobby has backed efforts to prevent sugar cane from being considered as a primary ethanol source while they acted to promote the use of corn to drive its price up; that had the predictable result, escalating food prices. I alluded to it before. Greed and self interest have replaced the national interest."

I nodded. "I see what you mean."

"There's a saying for it from the nineteenth century. 'Politics makes strange bed-fellows'. There are many more examples, but it has now come to a point where most Democrats will oppose most proposals by Republicans; and most Republicans will automatically oppose most proposals introduced by Democrats. The thousands of lobbyists make their alliances to accomplish whatever is in the best financial interests of their clients and offer support to candidates who will assist them in that kind of enterprise. In those circumstances, the national interest is the casualty. This is a most pernicious danger, one I saw even in my presidency, and it disturbed me even then, and it has been obvious for years to many of our prior political leaders."

"I wish one of them had said something."

"One of them did." The president grinned. "I warned the nation that it needed to maintain its unity as a nation of Americans, and that political groups would try to place their interests above those of the nation as a whole, but no one seems to have paid any attention to the warning."

I was puzzled by what Washington said. After I apologized for not being able to recall what warning he gave or when he gave it, I asked, "What exactly did you say and when did you say it?"

Washington smiled. "You may not know this, but I was urged to seek a third term near the end of my second term in office. Declining was a difficult decision. I wanted to retire, but felt there was so much still to be done to assure the continued existence of our fledgling republic. I worked very hard preparing a long Farewell Address in which I attempted to give the best advice I could to my fellow countrymen." President Washington sighed a moment. "This is exactly what I said about the dangers inherent in the division of our people into separate groups in 1796:

> *'... all combinations and associations, under whatever plausible character, with the real design to direct, control, counteract, or awe the regular deliberation and action of the constituted authorities, are destructive of this fundamental principle, and of fatal tendency. They serve to organize faction, to give it an artificial and extraordinary force; to put, in the place of the delegated will of the nation the will of a party, often a small but artful and enterprising minority of the community; and, according to the alternate triumphs of different parties, to make the public administration the mirror of the ill-concerted and incongruous projects of faction, rather than the organ of consistent and wholesome plans digested by common counsels and modified by mutual interests.*

> *However combinations or associations of the above description may now and then answer popular ends, they are likely, in the course of time and things, to become potent engines, by which cunning, ambitious, and unprincipled men will be enabled to subvert the power of the people and to usurp for themselves the reins of government, destroying afterwards the very engines which have lifted them to unjust dominion.'*

I had a little difficulty with the language of the late eighteenth century, but the meaning was clear and prophetic. I said, "You're right, Mr. President. It's just as you said. Small, artful and enterprising factions are being used by cunning, ambitious and unprincipled men to subvert the common interest."

"Yes. Greed and a desire for power pervade everything now, not just in government, but everywhere. Look at Enron. Look at executive compensation in the publicly owned corporations. Look at the pension and retirement benefits they award to themselves. Corporate mergers occur for no purpose other than to advantage a small band of corrupt executives. It's disgraceful. The same greed and lust for power seem to have invaded government functions. Corporations like Halliburton dealing with the federal government, even in places like Iraq where American troops are dying in furtherance of a now unpopular war, see it as a profit-making opportunity. Writers from the left, the right and from venerable publications like the New York Times and many news networks have raised questions about those activities, public and private, and our political leaders and the small public stockholders of the corporations fail to do anything. The problem continues. The general population of voters and small shareholders, many of whom know little of the disgraceful behavior of their elected officials are busy with their own lives. They have neither the time nor power to do very much. They all rely on their elected political leaders and their representatives on the boards of business corporations to properly act as a watchdog. But instead, their leaders and representatives betray that trust. In business, the business bureaucrats divide up the financial benefits and disregard what's best for the business and its owners and the nation that made their success possible. In government, the leaders prefer to deal with special interest groups to amass the funds necessary to perpetuate themselves in office and spend their time quarrelling with their political opponents, rather than in furtherance of the public interest. They prefer to divide the people and promote a class war of the poor against the rich and black against white, rather than work to secure equal opportunity for all." Washington scowled. "They are both more like a pack of hyenas dividing carrion than a watchdog". Washington scowled again as he said, "It sometimes reminds me of the decline of Imperial Rome. They should have been concerned with the threat posed by the barbarians, but instead, they had circuses to distract the people. In your time, Congress has hearings and investigations about inconsequential things like drug use by professional athletes rather than facing the real issues of the day."

President Washington paused a moment. I seized that opportunity to say, "I agree with you, sir. It is very discouraging, but...."

Before I could say anything more, Washington said, "Yes, it is. The way it is today, to be a nominee of the Democrats, a candidate must gain the approval of the left wing of that party; and to be selected by the Republicans you have to be accepted by the right wing of that party. In doing so, the leadership of the parties work to make the extremes as popular as possible and avoid the real issues that concern the common interest. For example, they use immigration and affirmative action issues to pit one group against another instead of intelligently dealing with the problems. They spend their time attacking each other on matters like abortion and gay marriage and other extraneous issues like those instead of the real issues like energy, the war against terror and the like. I ask you, just how important is it to the survival of our nation and the freedom and liberty of the American people that abortion rights and gay marriage should drive our political discourse?"

"I agree," I said. "In the grand scheme of things they don't mean much except to the people involved, but those things do need an answer. How can we prevent those issues from taking over?"

"We could make Thomas Jefferson happy and leave those issues of family to the several states to be resolved by the people of those states. There's no need to make those matters federal issues. What we should be discussing right now is how we get the federal government to solve the problems that are properly within its domain, not abortion issues and gay rights and things like that. Here we are, falling into that trap ourselves. I refuse to waste any more of our time on those matters."

"Okay, then just how do we get the government on the right track?" I asked.

"That's something you will help to accomplish," Washington said, "when you go back. That's why we're doing these interviews."

"How can I do anything?" I asked. The prospect of being expected to carry so heavy a burden frightened me. I protested. "I'm just a co-anchor on a local news program that's not even first in our relatively small TV market. You should have selected a news anchor from one of the major networks, not me. You need nationwide coverage. I'm terribly flattered, but I have to be honest with you. I'm not the highly respected news commentator that people throughout the country know and respect." I paused a moment. "I'm sorry, sir, but let's face it. Outside of my market area, I'm a nobody." I stopped and looked at President Washington. "Really, the important things you have said deserve a better advocate than me. I'm sorry, sir, but what can I do?"

Washington smiled. "We hope that truth will be recognized, that it will be accepted when heard, and that it will spread across the land. In my time, a little known pamphleteer, Thomas Paine, wrote a long essay he called *Common Sense*. It became widely read and helped ignite our Revolution. We hope you will have similar success." Washington paused a moment and then continued. "You are chosen because you are not considered as allied to any specific cause or economic interest. Say what you believe. Say it on television and on the radio. Talk to people you know and meet. I know you can only make a beginning. We hope that you will speak of these matters and other people will listen and discuss what you say. They will talk with others, and if what is said is right and true, many will register their dissatisfaction and demand change. Don't underestimate the power of truth."

Doubtful about the entire plan and my ability to be the vehicle to drive the discussion, I said, "And when am I supposed to start doing this?"

"When you go back."

"When will that be?"

"Soon, I hope, but not too soon, because we have more issues to explore."

"How long do we have?" I persisted.

"No one really knows for sure how long you will be with us. We talked about the energy issue first, because I think it's crucial for your survival. While you're here, we will discuss many other really important issues for so long as time permits. We could talk about unfettered immigration, campaign finance and the unfortunate decision of the Supreme Court that says that limiting the money raising and spending part of the election process is prohibited by the free speech requirements of the first amendment. I assure you that the people who signed the Bill of Rights never intended that result. Discussing what could be done to change that result and improve the electoral process is more than we can discuss at this time. There are other issues I will want to discuss, like freedom of religion and what that means." Washington shook his head, "There are similar Constitutional issues like the right to bear arms, that nonsense about Miranda warnings and similar perversions of our original intentions that we could discuss if time allows." Washington paused a moment and took a deep breath. "Yes, there are changes to the Constitution we could discuss, like perhaps a six year term of office for the president and members of Congress where Congressional terms are staggered so that a third of the terms expire every other year, and term limits for both. I'm not necessarily in favor or opposed to those changes, but we might discuss those kinds of changes to see if it would help reduce the influence of lobbyists by reducing the frequency of elections. We provided a method for amending the Constitution, and it wasn't by a Supreme Court rewrite, but we may not be able to get into those things and what I've mentioned is, as they say in your time, only the tip of the iceberg. Unfortunately, I don't think the reality of the current terrorist threat allows us the luxury of debating all of those issues. Our priority must be terminating our Mid-East oil dependency. If we get to nothing else, I'm sure that you'll do your best to impress the citizenry with the need to do the things we discussed to accomplish that goal. Now we ought to move onto a more immediate issue."

"What issue is that?" I asked.

"What do you think is the most pressing and divisive issue facing the country right now?" he asked.

"It's got to be the situation in Iraq."

President Washington nodded and then said, "I agree, and that's where we'll start after lunch."

5

While waiting for our lunch, the foursome I had earlier observed playing the eighteenth hole joined us. They had apparently had a drink after finishing their game and were still discussing the morning's good and bad shots in good humor.

President Lincoln sat down beside me, President Jefferson sat opposite him and beside President Washington. Presidents Eisenhower and Kennedy sat facing each other on opposite ends of the table. President Washington said, "You've met Thomas and Jack. I'd like you to meet two more of our members. Dwight Eisenhower, everybody calls him Ike, and I'm sure you recognize Abe Lincoln."

Overwhelmed by the presence of five of our most illustrious presidents, I was speechless. I stood and offered to shake hands with each of them. "This is truly overwhelming," I said more to myself than anyone in particular.

President Washington said, "The rules during lunch are that we can talk about anything, but everything is off the record. We don't want to detract from the seriousness of the main purpose of these interviews." After we all nodded in agreement, President Washington said to me, "Anything in particular you want to ask us?"

I thought a moment and then said, "Well, I don't know." I wanted to ask them how he and Jefferson as slave owners could get along so well with President Lincoln who abolished slavery and President Kennedy who championed civil rights for all, but was afraid to do so.

President Jefferson said, "You want to ask us about slavery, don't you? George and I kept slaves, Abe freed them and Jack was an early advocate for civil rights for the descendants of the former slave population."

"I suppose so," I said very softly.

"I know that our reputations have been tarnished. George was always opposed to slavery, but he believed if he freed them, they would be unable to care for themselves. They had no education or training that would enable them to be self-supporting in rural Virginia at that time." Jefferson smiled a moment. "The truth of the matter is that George really ran a retirement home for the elderly and infirm, rather than slave quarters. He freed them under his will because he knew there would be nobody to care for them, but many of them were owned by Martha and she didn't go along with George on the slavery question. My record, when viewed from current perspectives is less favorable than George's, but both of us reflected the mores of the times and the society we lived in. Abe had many of the same concerns George had when he freed the slaves. He was worried about their ability to care for themselves in the reality of the south in the middle eighteen hundreds." Turning to President Lincoln, President Jefferson said with a smile, "Don't deny it, Abe."

"I don't deny it," President Lincoln said. "It was a worry of mine. I even toyed with the idea of repatriating all the former slaves back to Africa as did Thomas many years before, but I knew, that as a practical matter, it wasn't possible."

President Washington interrupted. "I think we've exhausted that subject." Turning to me, he continued, "Anything else you'd like to ask or say?"

I thought a moment, "Only that I think it's wonderful that you are all so friendly and cordial."

"Why shouldn't we be?" President Jefferson said. "After all, my opponent when I ran for president was John Adams who was the incumbent. We had very serious disagreements, but he and I became best friends for the remainder of our lives after I left office. That's the way it should be. We should all discuss our points of view with courtesy and in friendship. I opposed Adams' Alien and Sedition Act, but he did what he thought was best for the nation at the time and I disagreed. I still think I was right and there are still people who think that Adams had it right. We fought vigorously, but understand each other's point of view and respect each other as patriots."

At the conclusion of our lunch, everyone else left, leaving President Washington and me alone. Washington said, "The topic for this afternoon is the war in Iraq. How would you like to begin?"

I thought a moment, and then said, "Let's start at the beginning. Should we have ever gone there? The war was started on a lie about weapons of mass destruction and most people say we should get out immediately. What do you think, Mr. President?"

"I hope the lie you refer to was the lie Saddam Hussein told the world."

It wasn't, but I said, "Of course it was."

President Washington smiled at me. "I'm not so sure of that, but it was diplomatic of you to say so. Recall that Hussein claimed that he had those weapons of mass destruction. People believed him and why shouldn't they? Beyond question, he did at one time have them. We all know that because he used poison gas against some of his fellow Iraqis and against the Iranians. US troops were exposed to chemical weapons when they destroyed an ammunition dump containing those materials at Kamisiyah in Iraq at the conclusion of the first Gulf War."

Washington scowled. "In an example of political reconstruction and back-biting, some of your politicians claim that President Bush and his administration lied to the Congress and the American people. None of us up here believe that. President Bush told the Congress what he and most of the rest of the world mistakenly believed was true and indeed was true at an earlier time. I'm not sure that was the president's sole reason for wanting to go to war against Iraq. Even here, there were members of the Club who looked at the successful conclusion of the Cold War and believed that the example of a free and prosperous society enjoying the advantages of capitalism was instrumental in persuading other Europeans behind the Iron Curtain to resist and ultimately vanquish the Communist dictatorships ruling their lands. We spoke of that before. They believed that a prosperous Iraq would be an example for its neighbors, showing the benefits of liberty and freedom the way West Germany did during the Cold War. Thomas Jefferson thought so, and so did most of our other members, including Madison, Monroe and Reagan. They all believed that people are essentially the same everywhere and they reasoned that a successful democracy in a Muslim area would similarly persuade Iraq's neighbors in the region to themselves embrace the kind of freedom and liberty you enjoy. As you should know, Abe Lincoln decided that bringing liberty and freedom to the slaves was a worthwhile addition to that of preserving the union as a goal of the War Between the States. Abe similarly thought that bringing liberty and freedom to the Iraqis was a worthwhile goal of the second Gulf War."

"Did you agree with President Lincoln about that?" I asked.

"Not entirely. It was a worthwhile goal in Lincoln's day, but that took place in our own country where we were better able to make it happen, and that took a long time. I feared that we did not have the ability to force democracy upon the Iraqis, and it now seems that the lure of liberty and freedom is not strong enough to make enough of the Iraqis want to fight effectively for it. In my time, Americans in the north and the south, with their varying economic, social and religious interests, all had a strong enough desire to achieve our mutual goal of achieving liberty and freedom to cooperate and make our compromises so we could live together peaceably. That seems to not be the case with the Iraqi people." Washington paused a moment before continuing. "My contemporaries knew that only by being united could we maintain the strength to remain free. I believe the nation should be eternally grateful to Abe for making that unity continue. Today's politicians profess to admire Abe, but they do not emulate his management ways. Abe surrounded himself with able, free-thinking advisers. He encouraged them to disagree with him and benefited from a full and critical review of his plans. Today's political leaders seem to prefer to surround themselves with sycophants and toadies."

"Do you see anyone today in the Lincoln mold?"

"No." President Washington apparently didn't have to think about his answer. After sipping his tea a moment, Washington said, "We digress. Let's return to the main subject."

I would have liked to have questioned Washington further about some of our current political leaders and asked him to compare them with Lincoln, but nodded in agreement and said, "Then do I understand that you think it would have been better to never have gone into Iraq at all?"

President Washington shook his head. "No, I don't think that at all. Saddam Hussein violated the terms of the cease fire to which he had agreed too many times to be counted. He continued to attack our planes. He tried to assassinate the first President Bush and he sponsored the use of bases in his country for the training of terrorists to be sent to the United States and other places. There's evidence that Iraqi officials at least knew and met with some of the 9/11 hijackers and I think helped them. There must be consequences for such behavior. We have repeatedly seen that the failure to respond to attacks by tyrants has dire consequences. Thomas Jefferson gave us an example from our time, and you are aware of the most horrendous failure to respond of more modern times which led to World War II."

"I'm afraid I'm confused," I said. "If attacking Iraq was not a mistake and staying there is a mistake because we can't change them, what's the sense of doing anything?"

"If the people of your time had made a realistic analysis of the situation and were prepared to expend the lives and resources in Iraq and Baghdad to make those places showcases that would demonstrate the benefits of liberty and freedom like West Germany and West Berlin did for the enslaved people behind the Iron Curtain, staying there would make sense. However, your leaders paid no attention to the history of the region and failed to understand or communicate to their people the difficulty of making so fundamental a change in the lives of the Iraqis. It probably requires a new generation of Iraqis to rid themselves of the tribalism and religious fanaticism that prevail there. There's no quick solution to those problems."

"Perhaps not," I said, "but the American people have indicated in poll after poll that they want our troops out of Iraq. Don't you agree that the president and the Congress have to listen to the people in a democracy?"

"In a democracy they do, but the United States isn't a democracy."

Stunned, I frowned and said, "What are we then?"

"A republic."

"Okay," I said, "but even in a republic, don't the president and the Congress have to do what the people want them to do?"

"Not necessarily. In your time, with the internet and world-wide instant communication, it would be possible to do away with Congress, and the way the current group operates, I confess that at times that sounds tempting. All decisions could be made by the people. The problem with that is that the decisions would be made based upon inadequate information by people, many of whom have neither the ability nor the time to devote to the analysis of the issues. You live in a complex world. People have jobs, families and distractions. That's why you hopefully select the more intelligent and more experienced people from amongst you to review all the information and make the appropriate decisions for the nation. That doesn't seem to be working all that well at the moment, but it's better than any other system we studied, and we think it still is."

I nodded at President Washington as I digested what he had just said. "Then let me ask you this. What do you think we should do? Stay in Iraq for as long as it takes or get out now?"

"That's not for me to say. The people of your time must make that decision for themselves; but, if the kind of commitment we discussed will not be forthcoming, and it seems not to be, then you must consider an alternative strategy."

"What would that be?" I asked.

"It's basically a policy of delay to buy time and hope that you will not have to fight that same battle under worsened conditions." Washington paused a moment, then seemed to re-focus his thoughts. He looked stern as he said, "First of all, we have to disrupt the terrorists whenever and wherever we can. Do you recall that earlier we talked about our hope that we would have enough time to end our energy dependency and stop funding the terrorists? We talked of stalling tactics. That's what we tried to do when we attacked Iraq, but we have to fight those battles in a way that suits us. If a modern day army were to wage war against the Mongol hordes of Genghis Khan, it would make no sense for that modern army to give up its airplanes, its tanks and trucks and machine guns and rifles for the bow and arrow and horses and swords. The Mongols would undoubtedly be better at that kind of fighting. That is what we do when we try to engage the Islamic fascists in a battle on their turf using weapons they have mastered where they employ a strategy that has time and patience on their side. As a military person during our Revolutionary War I learned that lesson. That's why I disagreed with President Lincoln and Thomas and the others about trying to force feed democracy to the local Iraqi population." Washington sipped his tea. "When we fought our Revolution, we were the insurgents combating a superior invading force. The tactics we employed then were similar in some respect to what the Islamic fascists are doing now. We didn't use terror tactics against the civilian population, but we avoided large scale, frontal battles. We attacked and then withdrew. It's an old and effective strategy to wear down a superior invading force."

"Then what should we do?"

"What we originally did was fine. If we were not prepared to expend the necessary lives and resources to force fundamental changes in the region, then, when the military action was concluded, we should have withdrawn. If Saddam Hussein returned to power, our air force could have bombed him from afar without losses to our people. If they continued to train terrorists or provide them with aid and comfort, we could bomb them again. We talked about that kind of possibility before with President Truman.

"Our goal should be to prevent attacks against our people and interests and buy time while we proceed with a plan to end our dependency on foreign oil. We can't impose democracy and a love of freedom and liberty on people who don't want it badly enough to fight for it. The United States does not owe anything to the nation that we believe was complicit in attacking our people. Simplistic statements like 'you broke it you fix it' are stupid beyond belief." Washington paused a moment before continuing. "We can also hope that fighting small battles on our terms along with the free world using its economic power will result in changes within terrorist governments. That strategy seemed to have worked to some extent in Libya and perhaps it will work in other places. Achieving that result while we avoid the necessity of deploying nuclear weapons is and must remain our goal. While that is going on, we can hope that an increasing number of people in the Middle East decide that peace, freedom and liberty are worthwhile goals for themselves. That has slowly begun to happen in different places in the region. In Kuwait, women ran for office and voted in municipal elections. Even in Saudi Arabia, women are looking to improve their situation and gain the right to drive an automobile. In Iran, there are young people who are increasingly unhappy with the rigid religious requirements of that theocracy. Those kinds of uprisings occurred in Eastern Europe, most notably in Hungary, before the Soviet collapse and they were brutally put down, but they persisted. We cannot make it happen. The people in those places must make it happen for themselves. We can only demonstrate that on balance, freedom and liberty are better than the crushing fascism of their ruling theocracy."

"Isn't that what we did in Korea, Viet Nam, Kuwait and Afghanistan? We attempted to bring democracy to people who were deprived of their freedom and liberty. Were we wrong in doing that?" I asked.

"They're all a little different. In Korea and again in Viet Nam, the main question was whether the Soviet sphere of influence should be allowed to grow. There's no use to second-guess the decision that the democracies had to do something. Eastern Europe was behind the 'Iron Curtain' and the Soviet threat to all freedom loving people was real. In Korea, Harry decided against using the atom bomb because of the risk of nuclear retaliation. I think he was right. He had very limited options, none of them very good. Viet Nam was a little different. Most members of the club and I saw that as mainly an internal dispute, first to expel the French colonial power and then a struggle by those rebellious people to establish their own government. Perhaps you don't know this, but the revolutionaries who wanted independence from France first turned to the United States for assistance. They even cited our Declaration of Independence in listing their grievances."

"I didn't know that," I said.

Washington paused a moment to pour himself a cup of tea from the fresh pot of tea in front of him, "Did you know that Ho Chi Minh had lived in the very city in which you work?"

I shook my head. "In Boston? No, I didn't."

"He did. If memory serves, he worked in that old hotel at the corner of Tremont and School Streets. It's still there."

"The Parker House?" I said.

"That's it," Washington said with a smile. "Because of our close ties to the French, we did not support the revolutionaries who wanted freedom from French colonial rule. We refused to help, because of pressure from France. It was Harry Truman that turned them down." Washington shook his head and sighed. "That was a mistake and Harry will admit it. Because of that mistake, the revolutionaries turned to the Soviets for assistance and adopted totalitarian communism as their form of government. I am convinced that if the US government had supported the rebels in opposing the return of French colonialism, Viet Nam would have been a freedom and liberty loving country and a strong ally in the current war against terrorism. Jack Kennedy inherited the situation in Viet Nam and he would tell you if he were with us right now, that he would have ended our military presence there during his second term in office."

I had carefully followed President Washington's analysis of the Viet Nam situation. I was a very young man during that era and thought I remembered everything about it, but I had never considered it in the way Washington explained it. I had to think about it some more, but it seemed to me that he probably had it exactly right. "Interesting," I said. "It would have changed a lot of things if we hadn't taken over for the French."

President Washington nodded. "The worst result from that era was that it popularized a philosophy of civil disobedience that resulted in many of our young people becoming opposed to our government and our laws. It's true that the young people were right and the government was wrong, but it sponsored extreme divisiveness among us and resulted in civil disobedience becoming an acceptable way of protest. Emotional and rabid action displaced rational discussion of the issues with the result that the correctness of the decision ceased being the issue. Pushing and shoving from one side led inevitably to more pushing and shoving from the opposite direction. Instead of rationally re-examining our position and correcting our error, the position hardened. As a result, we stayed much longer than we should have in Viet Nam and thousands of our people lost their lives." Washington shook his head sadly and then continued. "There's no need to bewail that mistake any further. I can only hope the people have learned something from the errors."

Washington paused a moment and then said. "Let's move on. You also asked about Kuwait and Afghanistan. The first Gulf War resulted from Iraq's invasion of another country. We, along with most of the free world, decided that we could not allow that to happen. We did what we had to do and ended that occupation of Kuwait by Iraq. We did not occupy Kuwait or Iraq. Some felt we should have gone on and taken Baghdad and deposed Saddam Hussein. That would have been acceptable, provided we immediately left the country."

"You mentioned it before and I know you have little regard for them, but what do I say to those people who say, 'You broke it, you fix it.'"

"It's nonsense. The first time we went to Iraq it was because they invaded Kuwait. We owed the aggressor nothing. If they had then established a government that wanted our assistance and demonstrated an ability to properly govern, I'm sure assisting them would have been appropriate. The second time we invaded Iraq, it was because they had continued to attack our interests. They defied the terms of the cease fire and claimed that they had weapons of mass destruction which they threatened to use. We do not owe Iraq or anyone else anything although we will always remain willing to help those who want our help if they are also willing to help themselves." Washington frowned. "I have no patience with well-meaning but uninformed simple-minded people who make decisions based on 'cute' little slogans like 'You broke it, you fix it'. I think it was

General Colin Powell who first made that statement as part of his effort to dissuade the younger President Bush from occupying Iraq. After that effort failed, it was improperly used to justify continuing the occupation. It seems to be a failing of the times that people in power refuse to acknowledge that they were ever mistaken."

President Washington pulled out his pocket watch, opened the cover and then said, "But enough about Iraq. You also asked about Afghanistan. That was also different. The September 11, 2001 attack was planned and directed from Afghanistan by Osama Bin Laden. Beyond any question, Afghanistan gave aid, comfort and assistance to Bin Laden. The United States had to retaliate. I would have done it differently, but I have no real quarrel with what was done there."

"What would you have done differently?"

"I would have had to discuss it with the operational commanders, but I would have suggested a plan utilizing our strength in the air. I would have gone forward with a ground war only as a last resort. We should have learned from the Russian experience in Afghanistan that a land campaign on that terrain should be avoided."

"So exactly what would you have suggested?" I asked.

"I would have located where Osama bin Laden was as exactly as I could and then used a properly sized tactical neutron bomb to kill him and his followers."

"That's some kind of nuclear weapon, isn't it?"

"Yes, but it minimizes blast and heat and kills with high radiation that dissipates very rapidly."

"Wouldn't some innocent civilians be killed? I asked.

President Washington nodded grimly. "Yes, some probably would, but far fewer than the three thousand or so of your countrymen who were killed on September 11."

"So you wouldn't have sent troops in to defeat the Taliban and take Kabul?"

"I might have, depending on our assessment of how much the opposition to the Taliban was willing to do for themselves. If we indicate we are willing to die to deliver freedom to them, why should they do anything for themselves?"

"You're absolutely right," I said. "Everything you say seems so right. Sometimes I have a view on an issue that is different than yours, but after listening to you for only a few minutes, I find my opinions are reversed. It may not be very professional of me, but I have to say that you are the wisest man there ever was."

Washington laughed. "Thank you, but no, I can make mistakes. We watch, we listen and we reason. We make decisions based on that. Many of the leaders of your time do the reverse. They make a decision and then they amass the reasons for that decision. Perhaps they do that because so many of them are lawyers. We think that's backwards." Washington sighed and paused a moment. "They act as advocates rather than as judges." Washington smiled a moment. "What I have is experience, a good memory and a group of friends and advisers who are motivated by a desire to do the right things at all times. The troublesome mountains of problems you and your contemporaries must climb are new mountains, but experience at climbing other similar mountains is a valuable thing to have. Look at history. It can teach you a great deal." Washington poured himself another cup of tea. "You haven't asked about it, and I'm not sure I've finalized my position as yet, but the situation in Pakistan is truly worrisome. The country is rife with religious fanaticism. We have no idea who will ultimately prevail there, the present government, moderates or the fanatics. If the religious fanatics pledged to *jihad* and Osama bin Laden prevail, we have to recognize they will have nuclear weapons, nuclear technology and delivery system capability they can use themselves or furnish to like minded fanatics. In the event the fanatics succeed, we will have some very difficult decisions to make and we will need to make them very quickly. Do we preemptively attack them with nuclear weapons and hope that makes retaliation impossible? Or, do we hope that they will not use their nuclear weapons, respecting our ability to retaliate, as the Soviets did, when we know, as we previously discussed, they do not fear death the way we and the Soviets did? That's something I'm not ready to discuss right now."

President Washington pulled his pocket watch out of his waistcoat, opened the cover and glanced at it a moment. As he closed the cover and returned the watch to his pocket he rose and said, "That's enough for today. Be here tomorrow morning for breakfast at eight o'clock. The topic will be immigration policy; that seems to be a significant issue in your time and there'll be a little surprise for you at our usual table."

6

I arrived at the Dead Presidents Club a few minutes before eight and saw a man with a bushy mustache sitting at what I now regarded as President Washington's table. I stared at him, and while he looked familiar, I couldn't come up with a name. He wasn't sitting in either of the seats that President Washington or I was accustomed to occupying, so my view was of his profile. He noticed me as I began to approach and bounded out of his chair to greet me, waving his arms energetically as he shouted, "George will be a little late. Come and sit."

I looked at him full face. His hair was parted in the middle. He wore a pince-nez that dangled on a string pinned to the lapel of his jacket. He exploded towards me in one, huge step. With a broad smile and enormous, barely controlled energy, he pumped my hand up and down in greeting. I finally recognized him. I had seen that face on Mt. Rushmore. It was Teddy Roosevelt. I had always wondered why he rated inclusion along with Presidents Washington, Jefferson and Lincoln, but that was a question I knew I shouldn't ask. "Wonderful to meet you, Mr. President," I said as I approached him. "President Washington said he had prepared a surprise for this morning."

He said in a surprisingly high-pitched voice, "I've been called a lot of things in my day, but never a surprise." President Roosevelt guffawed loudly. "I'm Teddy. Not Franklin, you know. Hope you're not disappointed."

Before I could assure him I wasn't disappointed, President Roosevelt said, "Do you know why people called me Teddy for a while?" Not waiting for an answer, he continued, "People called me that because I refused to shoot a bear. That was because the bear was captured and tied to a tree by my friends. They meant well. They did it so I could say I shot a bear." He laughed. "They should have known I would never do anything so unsportsmanlike. It's amusing. I built the Panama Canal, championed women's rights, fought business monopolies and trusts at home. I expanded US influence in South America and kept foreign states out, helped force a cessation of the Russo-Japanese War, got the Nobel Peace Prize, and did a multitude of other things during my term in office." He guffawed loudly, pounded his fist on the table and said, "But what am I best remembered for? Not shooting a bear." Without pausing, he changed the subject and said, "George asked me to talk with you about immigration because he sees that issue the same way I do. I'm ravenous as a bear. Let's order something to eat and we can talk about that after breakfast."

"Is President Washington all right?" I asked.

"Perfect. He'll be here after we finish the interview."

The rule at the DPC seemed to be, even with Teddy, that mealtime was not a time for serious discussion. Breakfast was delicious. Teddy ordered a hearty breakfast, a large glass of orange juice, oatmeal, a rasher of a dozen slices of bacon and six scrambled eggs with four slices of whole wheat toast, followed by an apple, a peach and a half gallon of milk. I contented myself with a small orange juice, three slices of bacon, two fried eggs, an English muffin with raspberry jam and a cup of coffee. That was more than I usually ate, but I was eating more than I normally would at all my meals and I didn't feel like I had gained an ounce. I wondered if that was what heaven was really like.

During breakfast we talked about everything but immigration. After he finished his orange juice, he said, "You're a good fellow. My real friends all call me, TR, not Teddy. I'd like you to do that." Without pausing to take a breath, TR launched into another subject. "George must have spoken to you about the need to stop talking and make a commitment to a real energy program so you can stop sending money to the oil sheiks, part of which ends up in the hands of terrorists who want to kill all of you."

I nodded and said that he did.

"I agree with him, of course. That's a little like the situation in my day with the Panama Canal."

I must have looked puzzled at his statement, because he laughed loudly. I noticed that, like George Washington, he, too, had perfect, white teeth. He then said, "It's similar because we had politicians saying, ever since the Louisiana Purchase, that we had to find a way to send ships from the Atlantic coast to the Pacific. That became even more vital after we acquired California in 1848. It's like now with the energy problem. Talk, talk, talk and nothing gets done. We needed a navy and we started building one during my presidency. What was essential was a way to get them from one coast to another. I was tired of the talking and made the necessary commitment to get it done. Same with the excesses of the railroad monopoly, they were worse than the oil companies and Haliburton in your time. I busted them up. There was talk and more talk about the great, unspoiled wilderness and a lot of hand-wringing about how some people wanted to abuse it. During my administration we started the national park system to conserve our natural assets. There are talkers and doers. What the United States needs right now is more doers and fewer talkers."

After Teddy finished his bacon and eggs, he smacked his lips and said, "I eat a lot, but I lead an active life, always did. I had been sickly as a boy, you know. I had asthma and heart problems. I took nitroglycerin all my life. I could have led a sedentary life, but I chose not to. I exercised and built myself up. It's disgraceful the way the people of your time have become so spoiled and lazy and obese. I say you ought to enroll all the overweight youth in a compulsory national service program. It would benefit them and the country."

After TR finished his third glass of milk and wiped the milk off his mustache, he said, "I began my presidency as a result of the assassination of President McKinley. He was murdered by the terrorists of my day. 'Anarchists' is what they called themselves. One of them shot me in the chest during one of my campaigns, but they didn't succeed. I made a full recovery." TR smiled. "The anarchists didn't pose as great a threat as the Islamic fascists of your time do, but they were a major concern to us. In my time, we also had the industrial businesses wanting to open the borders to obtain cheap labor they could exploit. That was especially true about Oriental immigrant labor at that time, so the issues then were similar to what you are now facing. You don't call them Orientals anymore, I wonder why. Asians. Not important, we're meeting to discuss immigration, not that stupid 'political correctness' that your contemporaries are into. Similarities between my time and yours, that's what we're talking about."

It took me a moment to re-focus. "I agree there are similarities," I said. "The Asian immigrants you refer to had to cross the Pacific Ocean. Now, we have to deal with our 1500 mile border with Mexico that people can just walk across. That's a much bigger problem, don't you think?"

"Absolutely!" He punctuated his statement by pounding his fist into his palm. "I didn't mean to say that the problems are the same."

Feeling a little intimidated, I said, "What do you think we should do about our illegal immigrants? Do you think they should all be sent back to wherever they came from?"

TR stared at me for a moment and guffawed loudly. "Lincoln had a similar thought about returning all the former slaves to their home in Africa for a moment or two. He probably told you that himself, and if he didn't, Tom Jefferson would have done so because he thought about that during his time." He laughed a moment and then pounded on the table with his fist. Impossible! Impossible I say. Impossible for Jefferson, impossible for Lincoln and impossible now. Bad for the economy, too. Foolish idea, can't be done. That wasn't a serious question, now, was it?"

"It's been expressed as a desired policy by some of our present political leaders."

TR scowled. "They can't be serious. That's no more possible to do now than it was possible to send all the former slaves back to Africa in Lincoln's time."

I had never thought it possible to deport all the illegal immigrants either. I then asked, "What do you think we should do about our borders? I don't think a fence could ever provide a barrier like the Pacific Ocean, do you?"

"Certainly not," TR exclaimed. "A fence might help, but they can tunnel under it, climb over it and find ways to overcome that barrier. You do need to beef up border security. It's totally necessary. The border must be protected against illegal immigrants and potential terrorists." TR smacked the table again, this time with the palm of his hand. He leaned towards me and said, "You have to control your borders! That's undeniable, but you can't keep them all out. Allowing people into your country in violation of your laws breeds contempt for the law. You can't have that. I'm opposed to that and I would do whatever is necessary to prevent its continuation."

"How do you stop all those immigrants from coming?"

Teddy smiled at me as he said, "Don't misunderstand me. I don't want to stop all immigration. I'm only opposed to illegal immigration. I'm all for legal immigration. The United States is, after all, a nation of immigrants. You need them, but you only need the immigrants who want to come to the United States to become Americans, not Japanese-Americans, or Italian-Americans or African-Americans or Mexican-Americans, just Americans. That means they have to learn to speak English and learn about American history and the Constitution and owe their allegiance only to the United States. They have to be law-abiding and productive and not be on the dole. I'd give them five years. If they commit any crimes or fail to learn English and pass a simple test on US history or refuse to work for a living, deport them back to where they came from. That's what I say you should do. That was my position when I was president and I said so many times during my campaigns and after my presidency ended. I said it in a letter I wrote on January 3, 1919, only three days before I died. TR pulled a sheet of paper from one of the many pockets of his bush-style jacket; he then adjusted his pince-nez and read:

> *"We should insist that if the immigrant who comes here does in good faith become an American and assimilates himself to us he shall be treated on an exact equality with every one else, for it is an outrage to discriminate against any such man because of creed or birth-place or origin. But this is predicated upon the man's becoming in very fact an American and nothing but an American. If he tries to keep segregated with men of his own origin and separated from the rest of America, then he isn't doing his part as an American. There can be no divided*

allegiance here ... We have room for but one language here, and that is the English language, for we intend to see that the crucible turns our people out as Americans, of American nationality, and not as dwellers in a polyglot boarding-house; and we have room for but one sole loyalty, and that is loyalty to the American people.

Shaking his finger at me, TR continued, "That was nothing new in my thinking. In a speech reported in the Kansas City Star on July 15, 1918, I said:

We of the United States belong to a new and separate nationality. We are all Americans and nothing else, and each, without regard to his birthplace, creed, or national origin, is entitled to exactly the same rights as all other Americans.

"And before that, on December 1, 1917, the same newspaper published these remarks of mine:

"Never under any condition should this Nation look at an immigrant as primarily a labor unit. He should always be looked at primarily as a future citizen and the father of other citizens who are to live in this land as fellows with our children and our children's children. Our immigration laws, permanent or temporary, should always be constructed with this fact in view.

"No one could ever accuse me of being anti-immigration, because even before that, I said this in a speech I gave on October 12, 1915:

We cannot afford to continue to use hundreds of thousands of immigrants merely as industrial assets while they remain social outcasts and menaces any more than fifty years ago we could afford to keep the black man merely as an industrial asset and not as a human being. We cannot afford to build a big industrial plant and herd men and women about it without care for their welfare. We cannot afford to permit squalid overcrowding or the kind of living system which makes impossible the decencies and necessities of life. We cannot afford the low wage rates and the merely seasonal industries which mean the sacrifice of both individual and family life and morals to the industrial machinery."

TR made an unaccustomed pause in his statement and then said, as if he had just had this thought for the first time, "The Europeans allowed a lot of immigrants into their countries after the end of World War II. Those people were regarded as mere industrial assets. They kept their foreign ways and lived separate and apart from their other citizens. It took place very significantly in France and Germany, actually all over Europe. They didn't want them to become citizens.

They did all the things that I said we should never do. They are having terrible problems with minorities in those countries, mainly Muslims, all over Europe."

I had been impressed as President Roosevelt recited what his historical position had been in that sharp, staccato way of speaking he used and said so.

He clapped me on the back. "Bully for you my man. I was never, in terms of today, a 'flip-flopper,' but that doesn't mean one should never change his mind. Have to do that when you're wrong about something."

I took advantage of a slight pause to ask him about schooling for immigrants.

"Good for you," he said. "I spoke of that long ago. You could look it up. It was in the New York Times on September 17, 1917. I said:

> 'We should provide for every immigrant, by day-schools for the young and night-schools for the adult, the chance to learn English; and if after, say, five years he has not learned English, he should be sent back to the land from whence he came…. We should demand full performance of duty from them. Every man of them should be required to serve a year with the colors, like our native-born youth, before being allowed to vote. Nothing would do more to make him feel an American among his fellow Americans, on an equality of rights, of duties, and of loyalty to the flag'".

"Would you give them driver's licenses?" I asked.

"Certainly, if they can pass the driving test. They have to be able to earn a living. I think my position is clear and it seems to me that the present government ought to act and do so immediately". President Roosevelt shook his head slowly from side to side. "I don't know how your generation puts up with that do-nothing bunch you keep electing to Congress. If I had been president of the United States at any time during the last sixty years, you would have 50 to 100 thorium powered nuclear generating facilities across the country and we would be exporting power to Canada and Mexico."

"Perhaps so," I said, "but there would have been one enormous fight with the environmentalists."

TR smiled. "I would never back away from a good fight, but my record as the first and foremost presidential environmentalist would preclude any serious attack. Anyone with half a brain knows protecting the environment was something I did before anybody ever coined the word. I created the first National Park at Crater Lake in Oregon in 1902. Then I created four others, plus 51 wildlife refuges. I passed the Antiquities Act that lead to the creation of 18 national monuments and I got the National Park Service established." He looked up and said as he spotted President Washington walking towards us, "Here comes George.

I'll be off now for a long walk. I've been sitting still too long. Might even play some golf, if I can find anyone to play with me."

President Roosevelt rose from his chair, bounded across the dining room and intercepted President Washington about half way between the entrance to the dining room and our table. They talked amiably for a few moments, and after a few hearty back slaps, a hand shake and a loud guffaw or two, they shook hands again and TR left. As President Washington approached the table, I started to rise to greet him, but he waved at me to remain seated. President Washington said, "I understand you and TR had a pleasant conversation. Do you need a few minutes to rest up? Most people do after spending any time with him."

"No, no," I said, "but he certainly is a high energy person."

"Yes, he talks very fast and can be hard to follow because he can go from one topic to another almost non-stop."

"I noticed that."

"What's more," President Washington said, "he thinks even faster than he talks."

"I noticed that," I said, "but he's an extremely interesting and likable person."

"Most would agree with you."

My journalists training kicked in and I said, "Most, but not all. Who doesn't think so and why?"

President Washington responded. "Often, he doesn't pay any attention to what people say to him, even when they are criticizing him for something he did."

"What kind of things?" I asked.

Washington smiled wryly. "A perfect example is what he did to obtain the Panama Canal."

I was surprised to hear that. "What was the objection there? I thought everyone was in favor of having a canal connect the Atlantic and Pacific."

"Everyone was. It was what he did to make it happen."

Puzzled, I said, "What did he do?"

"It took a revolution."

My face betrayed my confusion.

"At that time, what is now Panama, was part of Colombia. President after president attempted to make a satisfactory arrangement with Colombia to build a canal through what is now Panama without success. TR played a role in supporting a revolution that resulted in a Panamanian claim of independence. He quickly recognized the new government and made an arrangement with that government so the canal could get built."

"That is a bit extreme, I suppose."

"TR was accused of being an imperialist and lost some popularity because of his having done that."

"I'm not surprised," I said.

"Well, they had had something like fifty-three revolutions in fifty-three years in that part of Columbia prior to the revolution that resulted in their independence and the canal was necessary for the defense of the country. I think he did the right thing."

"Is he well-liked by the other presidents?" I asked.

"Oh, yes, very much. Why do you ask?"

"He said kind of a funny thing."

"Oh, what was that?"

"From what he said, it sounded like no one wants to play golf with him."

President Washington laughed. "Everyone loves TR. He's extremely smart. Between us, I think he's even smarter than Thomas Jefferson, and he's a real patriot who loves the United States and its people, a very compassionate man, but he can be irritating at times. When he plays golf, he insists on walking and carrying his own bag, and he walks so fast, no one can keep up with him. A lot of us ride in carts and the walkers like to walk together and talk while they walk. That's hard to do with Teddy. He marches right along, as if he were taking San Juan Hill again, talking incessantly, thinking great thoughts, enjoying the walk and the outdoors as much if not more than the game and no one else can get a word in. However, he is one of the best liked and most respected members of the club."

"He said that if he had been the president at anytime during the last 60 years or so, the country would now be getting all of its electricity from thorium fueled nuclear facilities."

"He's sure he would have done just that."

I frowned and shook my head. "That combination of environmentalists and oil and energy companies present an obstacle that I think he underestimates. The Congress and the various state governments would have all been roadblocks because no one would cooperate."

"Perhaps, but he would have tried. He'd do some things that he might or might not have gotten away with. He would not be subtle."

Puzzled, I asked, "Do you know what he would have tried to do? Perhaps that would be something we could do now."

"Knowing him as well as I do, I think I know exactly what he would do. He would declare the energy problem to be a national emergency and build those plants on federal land."

"How could he do that? That can't be right."

Washington smiled. "TR had a unique management style as President. He believes that, if it's not expressly forbidden, he can do it. He drives Jefferson crazy as Thomas believes the government only has the powers that are expressly given to it in the Constitution. They actually get along very well together most of the time, because they are both so bright, but on the rare occasions when they get upset with each other, TR says Thomas is really an anarchist in hiding and Thomas tells TR that he's a secret fascist." President Washington laughed a moment. "Neither, of course is accurate."

"I'm sorry, but I can't believe he could actually do what he said. For example, California has laws prohibiting the construction of any nuclear plant in the state. Congress would be pressured by lobbyists and voters to stop it. Look at what happened in New Hampshire with the 'Clamshell Alliance' that opposed a nuclear plant there."

"If he did it on federal land, the state governments would be powerless to stop him, and why should they or Congress even want to stop him. The current group in Congress may not be all that intelligent, but they have to really know that nuclear energy has to become a reality. He would take the criticism from those who thought they had to object because of their constituents and pay no attention to it."

"There would be people screaming impeachment."

"It wouldn't faze TR for a minute. The votes necessary to remove him from office could never be put together and he would know that. The only way he could be prevented from doing it would be if the Supreme Court decided he had exceeded his powers. If he had been the president on September 11, 2001, and did it then, I doubt that even the Supreme Court would have tried to stop him. As I said before, TR is a very intelligent man and a prolific reader. He used to read one or two books a day, maybe more. He would have picked a time to start building those facilities when he could be assured of having public support."

I thought about what President Washington had just said, nodded in agreement and had to agree. "If anyone could pull it off, I guess it would be President Teddy Roosevelt."

Washington nodded in agreement. "I think we might end today's interview now. I don't want to tire you out too much, and listening to TR is exhausting. Let's meet here tomorrow for lunch at noon. We can start the interview with Affirmative Action."

7

President Washington was waiting for me at our usual table when I arrived at the DPC dining room. As I walked towards him, I heard someone say, "He's looking a little better today. His color has improved and his breathing seems more relaxed." It was a voice I didn't recognize.

Another voice said, "I agree, doctor," in a familiar voice, but I couldn't put a name to the voice. The next second, the voices disappeared and I was seated in front of President Washington in my accustomed place.

President Washington said, "You must have had a good night's sleep. You look well-rested this morning. Have you decided what you'd like for breakfast?"

I did feel good and wanted to order a Teddy Roosevelt type of breakfast, but contented myself with my usual, more modest meal. President Washington had some kind of porridge and tea. During breakfast, Washington reminisced about the suffering his men had to endure at Valley Forge and about the admiration he had for the willingness of his men to continue their fight against British tyranny. He said that if he had it all to do over again there would be very few changes he would make in his life. He told me that one of his biggest sorrows was the early death of his step-daughter and one of his regrets was that he and Martha had never had any children, although, on reflection, he said that may have explained what some considered was his excessive love of his country and its people.

After breakfast, President Washington said, "Time to talk about affirmative action. There was a lack of unanimity among us at the club about affirmative action. Some of us, mainly from the south, perhaps because of a guilty conscience, were in favor of affirmative action for a limited period of time. As you know, I consider the continuation of slavery a stain on our otherwise almost perfect Constitution. However, it was compromise made necessary in order to achieve a unified government. The south could not be persuaded to give it up and the Constitution would never have been ratified if it had been prohibited. It took the War Between the States, and Mr. Lincoln's Emancipation Proclamation, which was probably unconstitutional, to begin to eradicate that blot. But let's move on. To understand our position on Affirmative Action, we ought to briefly discuss Brown vs. Board of Education decided by the Supreme Court in 1954."

Before President Washington could go on to start talking about the Brown case or Affirmative Action, I said, "Wait a minute, Mr. President. I hate to interrupt you, but did you just say the Emancipation Proclamation was unconstitutional?"

"Of course, everyone knows that. President Lincoln knew it. Slaves were property under the Constitution and the government couldn't deprive people of their property without just compensation."

"Who doesn't think so and why?" I asked.

President Washington smiled. "Teddy Roosevelt was one of the few. We talked yesterday about how he thought the president should find a way to do accomplish results that he believed were in the national interest unless it was expressly forbidden. Teddy says granting freedom to slaves in rebellious states was in the national interest and that nothing says it's expressly prohibited. President Lincoln was smart enough to claim the right to issue the Proclamation as an exercise of his war powers. He only freed the slaves in that part of the South that was still under the control of the Confederacy. Some people who supported the Proclamation did so as a temporary, wartime measure that would cause trouble behind Confederate lines. If you read the Proclamations, you'll see that they didn't apply in the Border States that stayed in the Union that still had slavery or in the counties of the Confederate states the North had already taken over. It took the 13th Amendment to finally end slavery, not the Emancipation Proclamation, but we digress. This interview was supposed to be about Affirmative Action laws."

I nodded in agreement and said, "I'm glad that we did. I find the history lesson very interesting, and I think it gives important background that helps explain the issue when you first explore the history of slavery."

"I think you're right." President Washington beamed at me. "Good. I think so too. Perhaps we should spend a few more minutes talking about slavery. We only spoke of slavery in the United States and of the black slaves, mainly captured by Muslim raiders, who were then brought to the new world mainly by Europeans. Slavery was widespread throughout the world at that time and it was not only black Africans that were made slaves. There were many others of all races. That bit of history doesn't excuse what was a shameful chapter of American history. It merely puts it into perspective. The reality of what happened after the War Between the States then necessitated the passage of the 14th Amendment that prohibited the states from discriminating against the former slaves and the 15th Amendment that guaranteed their voting rights. Unfortunately, the amendments were badly drafted and they ended up causing results that were never intended."

The Amendments were badly drafted and produced unintended results! Again, I knew that it was not on point, but my journalist training insisted that I inquire about that. I couldn't resist and I said, "May I interrupt you a moment, sir, to ask you to give me an example of the kind of unintended things it did?"

Washington nodded. "I'll give you one example, but only one at this time. The 14th Amendment was intended to provide former slaves born in the United States with the benefits of American Citizenship and declared that anyone born in the United States was a citizen. That now results in the children of all immigrants, legal and illegal, who are born in the United States having citizenship bestowed upon them, even if their parents have no intention of themselves becoming American citizens and they fully intend to return to wherever they came from, taking their children with them. We think that is quite silly, and it has resulted in a controversy about the deportation of illegal aliens who should be deported when those aliens have had children born in the United States. That's a problem you should not have to deal with."

Intrigued more than ever by President Washington's reference to poor draftsmanship and unintended consequences, I pushed my luck a little. I asked, "What about the 15th Amendment?"

President Washington smiled patiently. "All right. I said only one, but I'll give you one more." Washington took a moment to organize his thoughts. "The 15th Amendment was intended to secure voting rights for the former slave population, many of whom were poor, uneducated people who could neither read nor write. Many states enacted laws that were intended to restrict the right to vote of the former slaves by requiring literacy tests or by requiring the payment of a small tax payment. Rather than merely secure the intended rights for the former slave population, they did away with all those tests for all time and you now have a flawed voting population. I don't mean to sound anti-democratic to your 21st Century ears, but do you really want an illiterate, ill-informed voting population that can't read and write English electing your leaders? I think that was a serious error that could have been easily avoided by having that kind of reasonable requirement established for voting qualifications only be suspended so the former slaves could vote, and then take effect once more, after a reasonable period of time. Certainly, it seems to me that in your day and age, anyone that can't read and write English and who doesn't have a rudimentary understanding of our Constitution should not be allowed to vote." Washington frowned. "Just what kind of electorate do you really want?" He smiled patiently at me before continuing. "Do you think you're ready to begin the interview on Affirmative Action now?"

"Yes."

"Good. If we have time, we will return to discuss the 14th and the 15th Amendments another day if you have additional questions and, I assure you, there are many other unintended consequences."

I wanted to ask about the other unintended consequences, but knew that I shouldn't. I kept my mouth shut as I watched Washington sip his tea for a moment.

Washington put his tea cup in the saucer and then turned to me and said, "Affirmative Action seems to be an important issue of your time and I want to be sure we cover it before you have to leave." Washington paused a moment, smiled and said, "Now, as I said before, a sensible conversation about Affirmative Action requires, in my view, an understanding of what was done in Brown vs. Board of Education."

"That's the school desegregation case, isn't it?"

"Yes, it is."

"Do you think that was a bad decision?"

"Not at all. It seems very clear to me that separate but equal was a lie and that it violated the 14th Amendment even if the separate facilities were equal, which they never were and could never be. I'm in total agreement with what TR said at the turn of the 20th Century about the undesirability of our separating people by national origin or race, even if it weren't a Constitutional issue. The Supreme Court should be praised for finally overturning Plessy vs. Ferguson. After concluding that segregation by state law was unconstitutional in the Brown Case, the court then decided to return the case to the lower Federal District Court to remedy the situation. I and most of my colleagues believe that was a serious error. It raises the expectation that the Federal judiciary has the power and ability to remedy a situation that is far beyond its competence. A Federal judge has no educators, psychologists, transportation experts, social workers or any of the staff that's required to run a school system and, as should have been expected, unfortunate consequences followed. The federal courts in many places embarked on a busing program to force integration rather than simply prohibiting segregation. That was ill conceived. Even then, if they had started the integration program with kindergarten or primary school age children they might have had some success. As it was, it was a failure. It bred racial antagonism, destroyed the benefits of community schooling and a generation of school children in many places were political sacrifices to judicial incompetence. They received very little education and were ill-equipped to face the future. That was not a good result." Washington turned to me and asked, "Do you see how that leads into an understanding of our position on affirmative action?"

I admitted that I was confused and said as I turned my head from side to side, "Sorry, but explain it, please."

"Nothing to be sorry about. I've been thinking about this ever since the Plessy Case was decided and was irritated that the Supreme Court managed to mess up a very good decision in the Brown Case with that remand to the District Court. The remand suggests that the United States government, in that case, the judiciary, could right the racial wrong of segregation. It would be wonderful if it could, but, as I said, it was beyond their ability. Likewise, it would be wonderful, if through some magic, the harm done to the slave population by slavery and the segregation by the states and local government that followed could be wiped away, but it's probably not possible for the United States government to do that, and is certainly not possible to do that by giving advantages to the black population. Not every wrong has a federal correction. The Constitution should not be re-written by the courts to give advantages to blacks or anyone else for any reason. On this issue, the Constitution is very clear. Giving an advantage to one class of citizen over another for any reason is wrong and unconstitutional. It can easily lead to a decision to do the same thing for some other class of citizen at some other time. It's also, in the long run, a disadvantage to members of the class that receives preferential treatment. It's been said by many others but is worth repeating here. If you needed eye surgery, would you want to go to the black surgeon who was less qualified and got into medical school because of Affirmative Action? I think not. And how would you know? Might you assume, if he were black, that he got in because of Affirmative Action? And what about the black eye surgeon who is eminently qualified? He's probably thought of as being not as good as the other surgeons because it's assumed that he got where he is, not on his merits, but because of his race. That's unfair to that doctor. Supreme Court justice Clarence Thomas made that point in expressing his opposition to Affirmative Action and has been criticized for it. Even a thoroughly decent man like Bill Cosby who is generally opposed to shifting blame for problems in the black community away from the members of the community, criticized Clarence Thomas' position opposing Affirmative Action by claiming that he benefited from it. That criticism was unjustified in my opinion. After all, Clarence Thomas was an honor graduate of Holy Cross College and that is a very fine academic institution." President Washington frowned. "I don't mean to get upset at these things, but I abhor that kind of meddling with a perfectly straightforward requirement that says giving an advantage to someone by reason of their race is forbidden. Nothing could be clearer than that under the Constitution."

"I agree with you." I nodded and said, "I have to confess. I didn't always, but after listening to you, I've changed my mind. You've managed to persuade me to re-examine my views on many things I thought I knew."

"That's the purpose of these interviews. Not necessarily to change your mind, but to get you to re-consider things and re-examine your positions."

"Do you have another example, other than Justice Thomas? The controversy during his confirmation hearings about Anita Hill has made him an unpopular, and to many an untrustworthy figure."

President Washington shook his head slowly from side to side. "The allegation about inappropriate behavior she made was never proved, and it doesn't detract from the message in any way. Politicians allowed that kind of damaging and unproven claim to be used because they wanted to stop his nomination. That was unconscionable. No reputable news source ought to publish potentially scandalous accusations like that without corroboration, and there was a time, shortly before that, when they wouldn't have done so. The fascination of the media with those kinds of salacious claims is irresponsible. We, at the DPC saw that disgraceful, political show as an effort to destroy a basically decent man for having views that were different than their own. The law and his view of the law were no longer the issue. Politicians, pressured by constituents and lobbyists, opposed to his assumed views on abortion, turned a judicial nominating process into a media circus. It was assumed by them that since Thomas might favor banning abortions, his confirmation had to be prevented, no matter the cost. That fear did not justify their uncivil treatment of a person being considered for a high federal office." Looking very stern and unhappy at the same time, President Washington added, "What's more, in my view, the entire issue has no place before the Supreme Court anyway. Issues relating to marriage, divorce, family and criminal homicide, if you so regard it as such, are all solely within the jurisdiction of the states, not the federal government, as I and the other signers of the Constitution understood it. The tenth Amendment says: *The powers not delegated to the United States by the Constitution, nor prohibited by it to the States, are reserved to the States respectively, or to the people.* Nowhere in the Constitution does it say that the Federal Government has power over those relationships and acts. What's more, no matter where you stand on abortion, your position does not excuse the kind of uncivilized action in which both sides regularly engage. It gave birth to that kind of media frenzy that you now see far too often with irrational interest in the personal lives of celebrities from the entertainment or sports worlds or from the world of politics and government. It is a terrible diversion from your real concerns to spend so much time on those meaningless issues, and Congress does the same thing when it concerns itself with drug use by athletes or other extraneous issues. I know I mentioned it previously, but, honestly, why does anyone care when there are so many real matters of concern?"

President Washington sat quietly a few moments and I thought he had ended his discussion of Affirmative Action, but he hadn't. He said, "I joined Jack Kennedy for dinner here a few weeks ago. He had invited two guests, his brother Bobby and Martin Luther King. We got to talking about Reverend King's 'I Have a Dream' speech. You ought to read it if you don't remember it all that well. It's a wonderful speech. His dream was one of equality and non-discrimination, not of racial preference. It was about reconciliation, not of separation. He believed decisions should be based on character and on merit, not on race. I wish the black people of your time would understand that and stop thinking of themselves as perpetual victims whenever things don't turn out as well as they might have wanted. They should reject out of hand the efforts of those among them who always try to see everything as another example of racism."

I said, "There are law school and college professors who think financial reparations should be paid to the descendants of former slaves. They sometimes refer to what Reverend King said about collecting on the check that was written to them by the United States. What do you think about those opinions?" Washington looked at me, almost with disbelief as he shook his head. I was afraid that I had angered him and said, "I'm sorry sir. I didn't mean to offend you."

"Almost wearily, he said, "I'm not offended. You know I have little sympathy for people who lie by mischaracterizing something someone says or does. Saying that Reverend King was talking about financial matters in his speech is a total perversion of what he actually said. He was talking about freedom and equality, not money. The whole subject is ridiculous. If they talk about compensation, who is to pay it? The descendants of the families who owned their ancestors? Or perhaps the descendants of the ship captains who carried them from Africa? Maybe it should be the descendants of the mainly Muslim slave traders that kidnapped or bought them in Africa, or how about the descendants of the black tribesmen in Africa that captured and sold their ancestors?" Washington folded his arms and looked at me. He broke the building tension and finally smiled. "What they really want are for present day US taxpayers to pay for something they had nothing to do with. That might be good for some lawyers, but I find it beyond absurd."

President Washington looked at his watch. "I had thought we might cover gun control and the process of amending the Constitution this morning, but the discussion of slavery and Affirmative Action took more time than I thought it would. We'll get into that after lunch."

I apologized to President Washington for upsetting his schedule. Washington smiled at me and nodded pleasantly as he said, "I'm pleased that you did. It was very worthwhile, and it seems to me, that the people of your time, need to be reminded about what really is important and what the Constitution really says."

Martin Luther King was someone I had always admired, and I wanted to ask Washington if he knew what Reverend King thought of slave owners like him and Jefferson, but I felt that I shouldn't.

Washington looked at me and frowned. "You want to know what Reverend King thought about people like Thomas and me." He smiled. "You needn't deny it. Well, I'll tell you. He is about forgiveness and understanding. He understood that I was never a supporter of slavery, but he understood that I didn't believe I could oppose it at the time and get the Constitution approved, and he forgave everyone who truly regrets that sorry experience. That is what he believes and that would be his message to his and your countrymen today."

8

After another excellent lunch, President Washington pulled an old, handwritten copy of the Constitution out of his pocket and laid it on the table. He then recited: *"A well regulated Militia, being necessary to the security of a free State, the right of the people to keep and bear Arms, shall not be infringed,"* President Washington smiled at me as he said, "That's the Second Amendment to the Constitution." He paused a moment and then asked, "What could be clearer?" Not waiting for an answer, Washington continued, "When we wrote those words, we were concerned that some unscrupulous person might come along and, with a coterie of like minded despots, declare himself king and themselves royalty. We had resisted that and finally won our freedom from that kind of despotism. We were not likely to allow it to happen again. There was no greater unanimity among us on anything that exceeded our acceptance of that principle."

Washington paused and seemed to reflect for a moment. "Free people have suffered the loss of their freedom many times and in many places around the world as a result of armed rebellion. As you well know, military dictatorships exist in your time in many places. Another reason we supported that principle was our aversion to large standing armies. They can be taken over and used as an instrument of tyranny. The fear we had then was a real one, and it remains so in many places in your time as well. However, a sizable number of people in your time in the United States have come to believe the deviltry we feared is no longer a risk, and that the time is now appropriate for a change in the 2nd Amendment. Perhaps they are right. After all, in your time of tanks and rockets and other sophisticated armaments, a rifle or pistol would be no deterrent."

I nodded in agreement, but said nothing. I was firmly on the side of those who wanted strict gun control.

President Washington continued, "If so, there is a process for amending the Constitution. The people of my time were not so conceited as to believe that what we thought and believed during our time had to be the rule for all time. The process for making that decision is arduous, but has been followed on many occasions. It is not to be done by reversing the clear language and meaning of the Second Amendment, or by adopting unreasonable laws and rules and regulations restricting the clearly reserved right of the people. I have little regard for that type of artifice and legalized philandering. It breeds contempt for the established order and sponsors the philosophy that a desired result overcomes the law. Not even Teddy Roosevelt would have been that presumptuous."

"You said, I believe, that perhaps the proponents of gun control were right. Does that mean you think that the Second Amendment should be repealed?"

President Washington answered. "Actually, I think it should not be changed, but I could be persuaded otherwise. I understand that some in your time claim that the right to bear arms should be terminated because criminals have used firearms to commit crimes and murder. That has been the case from the very beginning. Thomas Jefferson said, quoting a writer of our time,

> 'Laws that forbid the carrying of arms ... disarm only those who are neither inclined nor determined to commit crimes. Such laws make things worse for the assaulted and better for the assailants, they serve rather to encourage than to prevent homicides, for an unarmed man may be attacked with greater confidence than an armed man.'

Arguments about guns only for hunting and recreational purposes miss the point. The danger is now and always has been from despots, whether they be motivated by greed, the lust for power or by religious fervor. In many places in the world, the government is powerless to prevent or is even in league with the criminals and despots. In the United States that danger does not seem too real; but, could it become a danger in the future? I will not refer to African or Asian nations or even South American experiences as you may regard them as having a different heritage. Instead, look at some of the European countries. Look at England and France with whom we have had the closest, historic affinity. As their radicalized Muslim minorities grow larger and more militant, may they have a serious risk of armed rebellion against the settled rule of law? Not at this very moment, but I believe they very well may in the not too distant future. There are groups within those countries working towards that very result. In any event, that's a subject for them to deal with. Could some religious sect in the United States now or in the future decide to impose their reading of their holy books or their religious dogma on everyone else by force of arms? That is a question for you and the people of your time to consider. Have the debate, but do it in a responsible way. Television sound bites, demonstration and marches are not the way for a serious discussion and consideration of important issues."

Washington paused to sip his ever present tea. I took the opportunity to ask, "Is there any more you care to say about gun control and the Second Amendment?"

"I think not," he responded. I think we should talk about another guarantee of what's become called the Four Freedoms of the Bill of Rights. Glancing again at the document on the table, but not reading from it, President Washington said, *"Congress shall make no law respecting an establishment of religion, or prohibiting the free exercise thereof; or abridging the freedom of speech, or of the press; or the right of the people peaceably to assemble, and to petition the Government for a redress of grievances.* That's the First Amendment. It's elegant in its plain simplicity. There were many of us at the time that thought the Bill of Rights unnecessary, as the Federal Government had no authority given to it to do any of those forbidden things. I've concluded that it was good to say those things the way we did because governments do have a predisposition to usurp as much power as they can. Right now, we'll concentrate on the freedom of speech part of the First Amendment."

"Being part of the media, I've always considered the free speech guarantee as the most important of all of our guaranteed rights."

"I agree that it is vital. Just as we looked at the experience of our having been subject to the British Crown and our experiences during the War for Independence as creating a need for the guarantees of the right to bear arms, that same experience base persuaded us it was necessary to guarantee the right of free speech. The speech we were looking at as necessary for the establishment and preservation of a free society was, of course, political speech. The Free Speech guarantee has been expanded from that to include all manner of expression. Books, movies, television, paintings and art, music, advertising and even raising money and spending it on political advertising are all considered as protected Free Speech. It seems to us that the Supreme Court has gone too far in protecting some forms of expression that have nothing to do with political speech. The people of your time should debate whether a change in that amendment is required to revise the way political campaigns are now conducted as we think the money raising part of the process is corrupting the government. Perhaps that could be done using the Federal power to regulate elections. The Constitution provides in that regard as follows: *'The Times, Places and Manner of holding Elections for Senators and Representatives, shall be prescribed in each State by the Legislature thereof; but the Congress may at any time by Law make or alter such Regulations, except as to the Place of <u>Chusing</u> Senators'.* Right now, however, I want to consider with you the applicability of the guarantee of free speech in your age of instant communication, where information can be transmitted everywhere so easily."

I was puzzled. Was President Washington going to advocate restricting that precious right that I believed was so basic to us all? I couldn't, I didn't want to believe that. I asked, "Do you believe the First Amendment Free Speech guarantee should be restricted in any manner?"

He sensed my disbelief and smiled at me reassuringly. "No. As I said, perhaps the power to regulate the manner of holding elections of Federal officials could be used to make a more sensible process than what you now have, but I'm referring to the communications that go beyond our borders. I believe that the right of Free Speech is basic to any free society, but not all societies are free or have our high regard for freedom. What concerns me is that the worst of what your society produces leaves your shores and does harm in other places and harms us as well."

Still puzzled, I said, "I'm sorry Mr. President, but I'm not following you very well."

President Washington nodded, then frowned and said, "I'm not being specific enough. I find the subject matter to be discussed very offensive and have difficulty speaking of it. The Supreme Court has determined that this type of speech is protected by the First Amendment, except for the very worst of it which is determined by standards that are extremely vague. Basically, I agree that the Amendment is so important to freedom that it should not be tampered with in any manner as it applies to communication of any kind in the United States."

I thought I knew what President Washington was talking about, but wasn't certain. He apparently found the subject so offensive he had difficulty saying exactly what it was that he was talking about. "I assume you're talking about pornography," I said.

President Washington nodded. "Exactly so. It has existed throughout the ages, and posed no real problem until recently. It is still not a real problem in the contemporary United States, but I fear it makes a problem for the United States in other places."

I nodded at President Washington. I was beginning to understand what was disturbing him. "Do you think we should debate amending the Constitution to except pornography from the protections of the First Amendment?"

"That's one solution, but one that I do not favor. As I said, I consider it so basic to freedom and liberty, that I'm reluctant to see any modification at all. The people of your time should understand, however, that the United State has an obligation to prevent the export from within its borders of those disgusting materials to other places. Ben Franklin is very expert in accessing what is available on the Internet and showed me some examples of what is readily available. It was a shock to my sensibilities." President Washington paused a moment and shook his head and almost shuddered, as if to clear a vile image from his head. He continued a moment later. "Just as we believe that foreign governments should try to prevent their inhabitants from exporting drugs or terrorists and their bombs to the United States, we believe the United States should try to prevent sources within the United States from exporting those disgusting materials to places that don't want it."

"It seems to me that drugs and terrorists are far worse than harmless pornography."

"They are. But is pornography harmless? In some cultures, primarily in the Arab and Muslim world, men and women are kept very separate. They do not go to school together. As you know, the women are kept sequestered and veiled. However, boys and young men are much the same everywhere. At a certain age they become interested in girls and biology takes over. The permissive way of life in the United States with its preoccupation with the salacious behavior of many of its celebrities is thrust everywhere. Especially undesirable to those cultures is the enormous supply of pornography that is readily available. That circumstance has had very unfortunate results, results that tear at the very fabric of those cultures in many places. Assaults, rape and other crimes occur in its wake, and they blame the United States, with some justification. Is the US government doing all that it can to stop the outflow of those noxious materials from our shores to their countries? I think not. It can well be said that no one forces the youth of those countries to look at the salacious materials; that it's their problem, not the problem of the United States. The same could be said about drug users in the United States, and that we should not insist on making efforts to stop the flow of drugs at their source. I'm sure you find that unacceptable. The United States should not say that it can do nothing about the exportation of materials that violate the laws of the recipient places because it would violate the First Amendment's Free Speech requirement."

"Do you think it does?" I asked.

"The First Amendment doesn't apply in those countries. If they determine those materials are illegal in their country, the United States should help them enforce that law. I don't think doing so would offend any important principles you hold dear. It's not like they would be asking you to enforce honor killings or some other deeply offensive custom."

I nodded. "I agree with you. We should try to prevent that garbage from our country going where it's not wanted, but is there a way to stop it? I'm not a technology maven, but it seems to me that the Internet is just out there and can be accessed by anyone, anywhere. How do we accomplish that, assuming the First Amendment isn't an impediment?"

Washington smiled. "I was hoping you would know how. I'm from the Eighteenth Century. I try to keep up with developments in your world, but I have no easy answer to that question, and neither did Doctor Franklin. Perhaps there is no perfect answer. But it seems to me that you ought to be able to do something. For example, there should be a way of discovering the identity of at least some of the people in Saudi Arabia copying that kind of materials and the US should cooperate with Saudi Arabia and other foreign governments that want to know who in their country is importing the forbidden materials. You should not refuse to cooperate with them because of the First Amendment, which those people are inclined to do, as if the First Amendment applied in those countries. There may be no total solution for the problem, but I would think you should exhibit a better understanding of the problem and do what you can to help those countries fight the purveyors of filth."

I thought about what President Washington had said. I had almost a reflexive resistance to any requirement that anyone disclose to any government the names of any recipient of information. Did I really want to ally myself with the "purveyors of filth?" I knew all the "slippery slope" arguments would be trotted out.

Washington could apparently tell I was troubled and trying to think through the issues he had just raised. He said, "Take a minute and think about it."

A little later, I said, "Thank you, sir. I needed a minute. Let me say, on reflection, I have to admit I agree with you. Why should we expect the Columbian government to join in our war against drugs if we refuse to help other countries in their war against pornography? Why should we expect help from Middle East governments with our concerns about terrorism if we show no interest in helping them combat the negative results they see from the invasion of their culture by pornography and other undesirable aspects of our culture? It's hard for me as a member of the media to accept what you say, Mr. President, but you have convinced me."

"Good. Before we suspend for today, I want to talk a little bit about another aspect of free speech. Free speech may sometimes seem at odds with the national defense. Frankly, I am appalled at the lengths to which the politicians and media of your day are willing to go to discredit the president and the government. It is basic to the Constitution that the people retain the right to criticize the government. There can be no argument against that. At the same time, free speech and the other prohibitions in the Constitution against government action, like the prohibition against unreasonable searches and seizures, should not produce a result that frustrates the lawful pursuit of government policies and decisions. Carried to an extreme, our normal reluctance to interfere with rights of free speech could lead to our destruction as a nation. Article 3, section 3 of the Constitution provides, *'Treason against the United States, shall consist only in levying War against them, or in adhering to their Enemies, giving them Aid and Comfort.'* It seems to me that some of the hysterical outpourings by some of our citizens during the Viet Nam era and again, during the more recent war in Iraq, can be said to give aid and comfort to the enemies of the United States, and therefore constitute treason against the United States. At the same time, we have a Bill of Rights in that same Constitution guaranteeing free speech that many argue says otherwise. The reconciliation of those conflicting views is the job of the Supreme Court. In our time during John Adam's term as President, Congress passed the Alien and Sedition Acts at a time when it was believed that war with France was imminent. The Sedition Act, passed in 1798, resulted in the fining and imprisonment of several newspaper editors who were hostile to President Adams." President Washington pulled a sheet of paper from his pocket, and before reading from it, said, "The Act stated in part, the following:

> *SEC. 2. And be it farther enacted, That if any person shall write, print, utter or publish, … any false, scandalous and malicious writing or writings against the government of the United States, or either house of the Congress of the United States, or the President of the United States, with intent to defame the said government, or either house of the said Congress, or the said President, or to bring them, or either of them, into contempt or disrepute; or to excite against them, or either or any of them, the hatred of the good people of the United States, … or to aid, encourage or abet any hostile designs of any foreign nation against United States, their people or government, then such person, being thereof convicted before any court of the United States having jurisdiction thereof, shall be punished by a fine not exceeding two thousand dollars, and by imprisonment not exceeding two years".*

When Washington finished reading from the paper, he pocketed it again and then said, "The Act, which expired by its own terms in 1801, was so unpopular, that it was instrumental in the repudiation of the Federalists and the election of Thomas Jefferson as President. The Supreme Court never had the opportunity of reviewing that Act, which is unfortunate, and Jefferson pardoned all who were convicted under it and repaid the fines."

I shook my head and said, "It seems to me that the law you just read to me was clearly unconstitutional as a violation of the right of free speech."

"Perhaps so. The Supreme Court had a chance to review a more modern law which you may well think also violates the First Amendment. In Schenk vs. the

United States, the Supreme Court tried to reconcile the conflicting viewpoints that free speech guarantees the right to criticize the government and that the government cannot allow people to try to obstruct its ability to carry out its appropriate governmental functions."

"I'm not familiar with that case," I said.

"I'll tell you about it. It was during World War I. The United States was at war with Germany and had enacted laws to draft young men into the armed services. Mr. Schenk was charged with circulating written materials to young men who had been drafted and accepted for service that told them to resist the draft. The government claimed that Schenk's participation in the distribution of circulars opposing the right of the government to enforce the conscription laws violated the Espionage Act of 1917. Schenk defended the prosecution claiming the conscription laws violated the Thirteenth Amendment that prohibited slavery, and, of more interest to us right now, that it violated the First Amendment right of free speech."

I nodded. "The slavery argument sounds silly to me, but the assertion that restricting his rights to circulate materials opposing the draft violates the First Amendment seems like a good argument to me."

President Washington nodded. "It's not an easy case, but the Supreme Court upheld Mr. Schenk's conviction. Mr. Justice Oliver Wendell Holmes wrote the court's opinion. He said:

'We admit that in many places and in ordinary times the defendants in saying all that was said in the circular would have been within their constitutional rights. But the character of every act depends upon the circumstances in which it is done.... The most stringent protection of free speech would not protect a man in falsely shouting fire in a theatre and causing a panic ... The question in every case is whether the words used are used in such circumstances and are of such a nature as to create a clear and present danger that they will bring about the substantive evils that Congress has a right to prevent. It is a question of proximity and degree. When a nation is at war many things that might be said in time of peace are such a hindrance to its effort that their utterance will not be endured so long as men fight and that no Court could regard them as protected by any constitutional right.'"

I shook my head. "That doesn't seem to reflect what is generally understood to be guaranteed by the First Amendment."

Washington shrugged as he said, "The opinion was a unanimous one and has not been repealed by any subsequent court opinion. It seems to me that unless it is repealed, it should be followed. I believe that the reasoning is sound and that, as a matter of necessity for your survival as a free nation under law, it should not be disregarded."

Washington paused a moment. I had the impression he could sense that I was not really happy with the Holmes opinion. He continued, "There are similar issues that have recently arisen about what is called by opponents of the procedure 'torture' and by government investigators as aggressive questioning. It hardly seems sensible to me to say that the government, under any and all circumstances, must conduct every interrogation in accordance with a set code of conduct that can never be violated. I like the test enunciated by Justice Holmes and would recommend it for your present guideline. There may be times when it becomes necessary to allow something which you might not allow under different circumstances, and that may include doing some things that some people call torture. I am not speaking of mutilation or beatings, but rather of other treatments."

I nodded. "I heard Professor Dershowitz of the Harvard Law School defend practices that I frankly found offensive."

President Washington nodded. "I also thought that what he said made good sense. If thousands of innocent lives can be saved by harsh questioning of a suspect, I would be all for it. The Bill of Rights, as Supreme Court Justice Jackson once said, is not a suicide pact. You may disagree, but I fail to understand how anyone can object."

"They fear that unless the government is restrained, they will abuse that power to question people; that they will profile certain people, discriminate against them and perhaps even seek them out and torture them."

Washington looked almost like a disapproving school teacher as he said, "It seems to me that fear of the government abusing its powers has led to the rejection of sensible efforts of protecting yourselves from danger. Calling something, 'profiling' and deciding that it violates some sense of fairness that is extolled by some of your politicians is quite foolish. I agree that governments tend to abuse their powers, but that is not a reason to prohibit the sensible use of them."

Before President Washington could say anything more about free speech, I suddenly found myself hearing a different voice, a female voice. I couldn't make any sense out of what the voice was saying. It was something about someone's blood pressure being improved. The voice then disappeared and the next instant, I was again sitting in front of President Washington. "Was there something more you wanted to say about free speech?" I asked.

President Washington looked at me quizzically for a moment. "You're back. I thought you might be leaving just as we ended the interview about national defense and free speech." He looked at me again. "We had a rather lengthy interview and I fear I have tired you. Let's meet tomorrow morning and we'll discuss freedom of religion and the anti-establishment provisions of the First Amendment. Presidents Jefferson and Adams will join us."

9

When I arrived for the next interview, President Washington was seated at the table with Thomas Jefferson and another man whom I didn't recognize. I assumed that it was President Adams. He was also dressed in the fashion of President Washington's era. Washington introduced him to me. "I'd like you to meet John Adams. He was my Vice-President and became the second President of the United States." After I shook hands with President Adams, Washington said, "You may recall when we spoke of the Alien and Sedition Acts of 1798 that it was John who signed those Acts into law, and that Thomas was very much opposed to those laws; and that Thomas then defeated John in the next election to become the third president of the United States, in large measure because of John's support of those laws."

Still unable to feel totally comfortable in the presence of President Washington, I felt overwhelmed to now be in the presence of the first three presidents of the United States. I could only nod my head and mumble a barely audible, "Yes."

President Washington stared at me a moment. "Are you all right? You're not leaving are you? We have important matters still to discuss."

I pulled myself together and said. "No, I'm fine. It's just that it's beyond anything I could ever have imagined to be in the presence of the first three presidents of the United States."

Thomas Jefferson smiled kindly at me. "When George, John and I discussed this morning's interview topic, we thought of inviting James Madison and James Monroe. If we had, you would have had the first five of us. We decided not to invite Monroe because he never said much publicly about religion, and decided not to ask Madison because his views are very much the same as mine, and there's no need for you to hear it twice."

President Washington turned towards me and said, "I know you well enough to know you want to ask Thomas and John about their positions on the Alien and Sedition Acts, but I'd rather you didn't. Thomas and John hold the same views today that they held then. Notwithstanding all that, they have become close friends and their letters back and forth reflect that friendship. When it came to religion, as you will soon see, they had very similar views."

That of course had to be agreeable. I nodded and said, "I'll confine my questions to the religion provisions of the First Amendment."

After breakfast, President Washington began the interview by saying, "It's useful to recall the exact language of the First Amendment and you'll have to excuse me for being redundant, but it is worth repeating." He recited, *"Congress shall make no law respecting an establishment of religion, or prohibiting the free exercise thereof; ..."* President Washington nodded, and then said, "It was well known and understood by my contemporaries that I would not countenance any manner of bigotry against Jews, Muslims, Catholics or any Protestant denomination or against atheists. I strived to create a nation of inclusion, not one of exclusion. Thomas felt much the same way and recognized and spoke of the dangers that are inherent in the way many act about religion."

Jefferson said, "I'd like to inform our interviewer of some background facts that led to the very simple language regarding the establishment prohibition. Prior to our Declaration of Independence, most governments everywhere had a state approved and sponsored religion and that religion, with very few exceptions, supported the divine rights of the king. At times there may have been disputes between the Crown and the religious leaders, but the relationship of approval and sponsorship of one with the other was generally the rule. During our Colonial days, there were many in our midst that wanted a particular denomination to become the state approved and supported religion." Looking at me, Jefferson continued, "That situation still exists in many European countries in your time. Even so liberal and forward a nation as Denmark has an official state supported religion to this very time."

I was surprised to hear that Denmark had an official state religion, but certainly wasn't going to challenge Thomas Jefferson about what he said. I nodded and said, "Interesting."

Jefferson continued. "When it became time to consider adopting the Constitution, there were some that wanted to have religion enter into the document in some official way. As he said, George wanted the Constitution to be a document of inclusion, not of exclusion. I agreed with him."

"As did I," John Adams added, "and as did all reasonable men. In our time, in Europe, most nations of the Christian world had laws which made it blasphemy to deny or doubt the divine inspiration of all of the books of the Old and New Testaments, from Genesis to Revelations. In England, any denial of divine inspiration was blasphemy and was punished by the boring of a hole through the tongue with a red-hot poker. In the colonies and in the United States it was not much better. In Massachusetts, near the end of the Eighteenth Century, the laws were modified, repealing the cruel punishments of the prior law against blasphemy by substituting a fine and imprisonment for that offense."

I was puzzled and asked, "Are you saying that even after the adoption of the Constitution and the Bill of Rights, those laws against blasphemy still existed in the United States?"

"Yes," Adams replied.

"How is that possible? We had the First Amendment."

"I know," Adams said. "I'll recite it to you again. *'Congress shall make no law respecting an establishment of religion, or prohibiting the free exercise thereof.'*" Adams turned towards me and looked at me as he said, "You recognize, don't you, that when we adopted it, the First Amendment prohibition applied only to Congress? It had no applicability to the several states of the Union."

I had read the First Amendment a million times. How could I not have realized it didn't apply to the states? "I always assumed that it did," I said.

President Washington looked almost amused as he said, "It does in your time. The Supreme Court decided in a series of its opinions that most of the requirements of the Bill of Rights are applicable to the states under the Due Process clause of the 14th Amendment. We're not overly impressed with the reasoning, but I know that John and I are pleased by the result. I'm not so sure Thomas is, however."

"No, no," Jefferson said. "My states-rights predispositions do not control my every thought. I too applaud the result. It's the reasoning that I find difficult to accept. The 14th Amendment states that, *'No State shall make or enforce any law which shall abridge the privileges or immunities of citizens of the United States'*; it seems to me that the privileges and immunities clause is a much sounder basis to support those conclusions than the due process clause. After all, the First Amendment says that US Citizens cannot be deprived of freedom of religion or have to endure the machinations of religionists as a result of any federal action. I regard that as a privilege and immunity of federal citizenship."

Jefferson wanted to explain his position in greater detail, but before he could continue, Washington turned towards Jefferson and said, "Thomas, I probably agree with you, but there's no need to discuss the matter any further. The result is a good one and this interview has more important matters to discuss than the poor reasoning in a series of Supreme Court decisions when we have no interest whatever in changing the results of those decisions. I'm sure you agree."

"Of course I do. We have to talk more about the First Amendment prohibitions regarding religion. Before I led us astray, for which I apologize, John had described the harsh penalties the law in some states provided for the crime of blasphemy, which included questioning the word of the scriptures. I am ashamed to say that the Virginia and Massachusetts colonies passed laws prohibiting blasphemy and authorizing the death penalty for violation of those laws, although I don't believe anyone ever was executed. Whipping and banishment were the usual penalties. Even after independence and ratification of the Constitution and the First Amendment, and where there was no law on the books prohibiting blasphemy, a man in the United States was convicted of blasphemy."

"How did that happen?" I asked.

"It was in New York, in 1811. A man named Ruggles was convicted of blasphemy even though there was no law on the books regarding blasphemy. The court said there need not be a law on the books, as blasphemy was a crime under English common law and was, therefore, part of New York's common law."

"May I ask? What did Ruggles do?"

"He disparaged the divinity of Jesus Christ." Jefferson smiled. "That's a similar kind of offense to that which occurs in your day and age, when Muhammad is belittled in any manner by anyone. As you have seen on many occasions, that results in hordes of angry Muslims calling for that person's death."

Adams chuckled as he interrupted. "It's a good thing you didn't live in New York, Thomas." Adams pulled an old letter out of his pocket as he turned towards me. He said, "I'm going to read one sentence from a letter Thomas sent me." Adams unfolded the letter, scanned it a moment and then said, "This is what Thomas wrote to me on April 11, 1823, *And the day will come when the mystical generation of Jesus, by the supreme being as his father in the womb of a virgin will be classed with the fable of the generation of Minerve in the brain of Jupiter.*' It would surely have sent him to jail in New York and possibly Virginia, if anyone had known of it."

Washington must have noted the confused look on my face. He said, "Sorry to interrupt, John, but I think our interviewer is not familiar with the old meaning of the word 'generation' as Thomas used it in his letter. It's defined as the 'act or process of bringing offspring into being.'"

"I thought that's what it meant, but I wasn't sure. Thank you Mr. President." I said.

Jefferson smiled wryly. "That's not the only thing I ever said that could have created a problem for me. It was well known that I believed there should be a wall of separation between church and state. It was not as well known, however, that in 1787, in a letter to a friend, I even said that we ought to be able to question with boldness the very existence of God; and four years after my term as president ended, I said in a letter to a friend, *'History, I believe, furnishes no example of a priest-ridden people maintaining a free civil government.'* Just recall that it was the religious leaders who often blamed witches and their enemies for whatever ills that may have occurred, and that they sponsored the practice of burning people at the stake." Jefferson paused a moment and then continued, "In another letter the next year to another friend on the same subject, I said, *'In every country and in every age, the priest has been hostile to liberty. He is always in alliance with the despot, abetting his abuses in return for protection to his own.'* I believed then and most solemnly now say to you and the people of your time, beware of the tyranny of the clergy. When they preach exclusion and that their way is the only right way, they violate every basic principle of our Constitution and threaten freedom for all. If you remember nothing else I have said, remember that."

President Washington nodded his head. "What Thomas has told you is especially apt in your time. The danger to you is mainly external from certain Muslim clerics, but, do not disregard the fact that the danger is also internal. There are people who want to make your dispute with the Islamic fascists into a religious war. As part of that strategy, they want to insist on trying to make the United States a Christian nation. They want to invest the scriptures with more power than the civil laws passed by Congress and the legislatures of the several states that comprise our nation. They want to conform the Constitution and man-made law to their interpretation of the Scriptures. I beseech you. Do not allow that to happen. Take Thomas' warning to heart."

"I have to ask," I said, "are you endorsing or opposing any particular candidate for political office?"

President Washington shook his head. "Certainly not. It is not the intent of any of us to dictate whom you should choose for any office. That question is one for you and your time. Just recall the lessons from history and from current events. Christianity has come a long way since the disgraceful historic events, like the Crusades, the Inquisition in the Fifteenth Century and, until recently, Christians attacking other Christians in Ireland. Your time is now experiencing religious based terrorism in many places around the planet. It's not only Muslims attacking Jews, Christians, Buddhists and Hindu, and those people retaliating; you also have Muslims attacking Muslims in the Middle East and Sudan. Often, the disputes have very little to do with piety. Religion is used as a rallying point to inflame the passions of the citizenry. Do not allow Christianity to become an issue in your elections." Washington frowned, before continuing. "I had thought those issues were resolved for all time in the United States when Jack Kennedy ran for president and was elected. Some, at that time, questioned whether his adherence to Catholicism and its Pope should disqualify him from becoming president. He made it clear that his allegiance, first and foremost, was to the United States and its Constitution and laws. I would insist upon the same undertaking from all candidates for any federal office." Washington paused a moment. "Please recall, that on accepting the office of president of the United States, the Constitution provides that the person so honored shall ... *'solemnly swear (or affirm) that I will faithfully execute the Office of President of the United States, and will to the best of my Ability, preserve, protect and defend the Constitution of the United States.'* It seems to me, that if any candidate cannot declare that the Constitution and the laws of the United States are supreme over any other set of laws or principles, including the scriptures, that such candidate is not fit to be president of the United States or hold any political office in the United States." Washington paused a moment to let his statement sink in. He then said, "Let me remind you of something. Clerics in Egypt brought about the assassination of Anwar Sadat because he maintained that the secular laws of their legislative body should take precedence over the *Sharia* laws of the Koran. I see very little difference between that and politicians in the United States in your time who claim the scriptures should take precedence over the Constitution. Both are incompatible with liberty and freedom in a free society."

I had no difficulty in agreeing completely with President Washington.

When our discussion of religion ended, President Adams and President Jefferson stood, shook hands with me again and wished me good fortune and a speedy recovery. Recovery from what? I thought their statement a little odd, but said nothing and only thanked them. As they walked off together in animated conversation, I thought they made a strange pair. They had been political enemies who had become best friends.

As they left the dining room, President Washington said, "It's strange. They both died on the same day, July Fourth, fifty years after the date of the Declaration of Independence. It is unlikely that such a friendship could occur with any of the presidents of the Twentieth or Twenty-First centuries."

I thought a moment. "At one time I thought that Bill Clinton and the first President Bush might become friends, but that didn't last very long, so I have to agree with you. I don't know why it should be so different. Why do you think it is?"

"It's partisan politics. In my Farewell Address, I made my views about political parties known. I always considered them a divisive force, one that could create animosities rather than unity. My fears were justified, as that is exactly what appears to be the case. In your time, the divisions have deepened. The parties are controlled by ambitious people who place party above the nation. Their internal fight to control their political party drives candidates seeking party approval to outdo each other with appeals to the extremes. Within each party, one-issue-oriented lobbyists insist that candidates accept their position or forego their support and their funds. When we discussed free speech, I was about to talk a little about the election process, but you had to leave for a moment, and when you returned, I felt you were too tired to continue the interview. We didn't return to it this morning because we had scheduled the discussion on religion and I had invited Presidents Adams and Jefferson."

"I'm ready to listen to you right now," I said. "How do you think we can fix the process? I certainly agree that it needs fixing."

Washington smiled at me. "I'm flattered that you hold me in such high esteem as to think I have a ready answer to so perplexing a problem. Unfortunately, I do not have an easy answer as to how you might best change the election process. If there were an easy answer, someone would probably already have suggested it." He paused a moment and then said, "It seems to me that the Senators and Representatives who are currently in office have little interest in changing a system that has placed them in office. Did I recite to you the provisions of Article 1, Section 4 of the Constitution?"

I wasn't sure what Article 1, Section 4 dealt with, or whether President Washington had recited it, and began looking through my notebook, as I said, "Sorry, it's probably in my notes, but I don't remember exactly what that Section said."

Washington smiled. "Stop your searching. I will recite it for you again. *The Times, Places and Manner of holding Elections for Senators and Representatives, shall be prescribed in each State by the Legislature thereof; but the Congress may at any time by Law make or alter such Regulations, except as to the Place of Chusing Senators*'. I think it might be timely for the president to appoint a committee of former Senators and Representatives to formulate a set of laws they might present to the Congress, so Congress might enact election laws that would improve on the sorry spectacle you now have. We didn't write anything about primary elections because we didn't have that process and didn't have the political parties like you do today, but it seems to me that the language I read to you about Congressional elections, and similar language about presidential elections, could be interpreted broadly enough to enact a better plan than what has evolved over the years. I would suggest that some of the leading Constitutional Law scholars at your law schools and some historians be added to the committee to help steer a proper course that will not violate principles of that document. That will not fix the system entirely, but it will make for an improvement."

"That would help," I said, "but it doesn't take the money and fund raising out of the equation."

"True, but what you suggest requires that either the Supreme Court reverses itself on a number of its prior decisions, or that the Constitution be amended. There's nothing to be done about the former and I'm not ready to advocate the latter at this time." President Washington paused a moment to look at his pocket watch and then said, "We ran a little later than I expected. Let's have a leisurely lunch and we can decide whether to continue the interview or suspend until tomorrow morning."

10

After lunch, President Washington and I decided to continue the interview. I said, "We've covered a number of subjects of current interest, but there's one we haven't covered, that, for some reason, seems to interest me especially, at this time. It never used to, but right now it does."

"It may reflect your current situation," Washington said. I wanted to ask him what he meant by that, but he nodded at me to continue as he said, "And just what is that topic?"

"It's the current healthcare situation. Most politicians say they have a plan to provide healthcare to everyone, but nothing I hear seems to me to be a solution to the problem."

President Washington thought a moment and then said, "I marvel at the advances in medical treatment that have been made since my day. The future may hold even greater wonders, but the cost of some of those advances makes the comprehensive solution for the health care assumptions that the people of your time are making quite impossible."

"What assumptions?" I asked.

President Washington looked down a moment. When he looked up at me again, I observed what appeared to me to be a rather sad smile. Washington said, "It seems to be assumed by the people of your time that everyone is entitled to the same excellent healthcare. That's a wonderful thing to wish for." Washington sipped his tea a moment. "Those opposed to the current system argue that the administrative costs of the health insurance industry are wasteful and monstrous. They say that too much time is devoted to administrative paper-work and not enough to patient care; that too many decisions are based on insurance company interests rather than patient interests. They are right. They also say that since healthcare is a basic human right, the same degree and quality of care should be furnished to all, that cost should not be a consideration, and that everything should be paid for by the government. As I said, a wonderful idea in theory, but it is wrong. It has been demonstrated, time after time, that the government is no more efficient or less wasteful than private companies. History tells us they are usually worse. Wherever it has been tried, it provides inferior healthcare with all of the problems of typical government programs." Washington smiled at me kindly. "Totally free healthcare for all, in my view, means reducing the quality of the services for all to a very low and unsatisfactory common denominator. It also means, because the government will resist paying for those services, that the government will insist that the providers of those services receive as little compensation as the government can get away with, and that is also wrong. Ultimately, that kind of poor treatment of physicians will ultimately lead to the best and brightest of your young people looking to other professions." Washington paused a moment and smiled at me, "And why look only to health care? There are other basic human rights in addition to healthcare. A decent place to live and food to eat are also basic to human life. Does that mean we should all have the same quality of housing and the same quality of nourishment? Preposterous! Yet, the logic is the same and that is what you get when you travel down that road. That kind of thinking destroys all incentives to labor and employ your talents to the fullest extent that you may. The biggest fault, however, is that it just doesn't work. It was carried out to an extreme in the old Soviet Union and its health care, housing and food were all inferior. Repressive force and secret police are then required to keep the peace. Only when that system was replaced did the lives of its citizens improve."

Washington sipped at his tea again for a moment before continuing. "Some of your contemporaries look to your neighbor to the north, Canada, as an example that the US should emulate, and say that medical care there is better than what you now have. Look to it and decide for yourself; but be aware that political figures in Canada that speak highly of the system there, themselves go to the Unites States and pay for health care, when, unfortunately, they are in need of care, and they do not wish to wait for the free care to become available to them. Do you want a system that requires that you wait months for some diagnostic test like an M.R.I., or perhaps even years for needed hip or knee replacement surgery? I think not. Our goal should be to provide equal access, not necessarily equal service. A meritocracy may have its faults, but it's better than the alternatives."

Washington paused a moment to fill his teacup. "I personally find it offensive that a society that pays enormous amounts of money for the performance of actors, musicians and athletes allows the government and insurance companies to dictate the amounts that physicians may receive for performing their services. I'm not at all sure that it can be supported under the Constitution. Skilled lawyers draw contracts the insurance companies require of healthcare providers, but, as I have said before, I have no high regard or patience for such clever, legal trickery. However, it seems to me, that dealing with healthcare is something the people of your time will have to determine for themselves."

"You can offer no further assistance?"

"You flatter me again by thinking I have solutions for all problems. I have none for that particular issue at this time. I can only warn you to be cautious in adopting any particular plan and that you remember that very often what is free is not worth having. What is often proposed for health care is promoted as comprehensive free health care. It will not be comprehensive, and it will certainly not be free. It will actually be very expensive to all in the amount of taxes that will be required to pay for what will most likely be a very unsatisfactory and inefficient health care system. Why the people of your time believe the government can run things efficiently, when it has been repeatedly demonstrated that they are even less competent to do so than private businesses, continues to mystify us." Washington opened his pocket watch, glanced at it momentarily, and said, "Enough of that. We should move on to the business world and the economy. The health of the nation's economy determines in large measure the felicity of its people. It's a very important subject at this moment in your time and I'm happy to say I have some suggestions that may restore my lost esteem for having nothing to say of merit on the health care issue."

"You've not lost anything with me," I said. "I could not be more impressed with anyone than I am with you."

Washington nodded at me. "Thank you. You're very kind to say so." He continued with a smile, "I hope my views on what should be done about the economy will not reduce your current high regard for me. Some of my views may be at a variance from what the intellectuals and pundits of your time treat as economic gospel. After all, I was a surveyor and then a soldier and plantation owner before I became president, and was not a particularly successful planter. Truth to tell, I had to borrow money so as to attend my own inauguration as president." Washington smiled. "However, I am no stranger to Wall Street. That very inauguration, interestingly enough, took place on April 30, 1789 on Wall Street in the City of New York."

Surprised, I said, "I didn't know that."

"Oh yes, John Adams was the first occupant of the White House. When I became commander of the Revolutionary Army, I insisted that there be no compensation attached to that position. I thought it should be beyond question that my service was tendered from love of country, and not for any financial benefit. I felt the same way when honored by my being selected as president and said in my speech on Wall Street that I would forswear any compensation beyond the recompense made clearly in furtherance of the aims of our new government. That thinking and pronouncement would not sit well with the denizens of that street in your time; but enough of that piffle. We have to consider the economy and business, and I tell you that tale to point out the contrast between what I did at my inauguration with the philosophy that rules that now famous street of commerce in your time."

Washington frowned. "The captains of industry now claim that they must conduct the affairs of their businesses to maximize the profits that can be derived from the business. In doing so, they say they need follow only the letter of the law and that it is their obligation to bend, stretch and even contort the law if doing so will enhance the amount of their profits for their shareholders. They say they need not trouble themselves with concerns for the nation that protects their business, their community, their family and themselves. I do not agree with that. What's more, I believe what they really are saying is that they will conduct the business under their stewardship to maximize what they may personally take from the business. I spoke before of my wonderment at your society that pays its entertainers and athletes so much while insisting that physicians with enormous talents should receive the small amount that government and insurance company functionaries determine they can get away with. I am similarly mystified at the compensation allowed to corporate officers. Greed and avarice have replaced humility, accomplishment and reason. You have only to read the Wall Street Journal for one month to become revolted by the incredible demands of so many corporate executives. What concerns me more than their greed, more than their corruption and occasional fraudulent transactions, is the total disregard of their country. As I said before, I am not an economist, and I know that the traditional thinking in your time is that the companies that produce goods and services should go to whatever place there is that has the cheapest labor and other costs so as to produce what they do at the lowest possible price. They argue that the people of the United States interests are served in that manner as the goods and services they require will be available at a cheaper price."

"Do you disagree with that? I asked.

"No. I agree that those goods and services will be produced at a cheaper price and that there will be some advantage to all consumers as a result. However, there is certainly no advantage to the persons who lose their jobs or the community that suffers the loss of a major business that had been located in that community. I do not agree that the policy is a good one, but I will accept the collective judgment of the politicians who make the laws that allow those events to occur and the people who elect them that such results and thinking is satisfactory. My concern is with the result those decisions have on the ability of the government to do the most basic of the things that are required of it. It is when that ability to perform its obligatory functions is frustrated that I would overcome my reticence to object."

I had become accustomed to President Washington's manner of speaking during the course of our interviews, but had a lot of trouble figuring out what he was talking about. I asked, "What government functions are you referring to, Mr. President?"

"The most basic," Washington said, "defense of the nation against invasion or insurrection."

I was going to ask another question because I still didn't get the connection, but before I could, he said, "We should learn from history. The United States won the War Between the States because the Union could produce all the necessary guns and armaments to do so and the Confederates could not. In more modern times, a similar result occurred in World War II. The United States became the arsenal of liberty. The economy of the free world out produced that of the Soviet bloc, thereby demonstrating the superiority of our economic system, and the Soviet Union collapsed from within. You know all these things. There's no need to dwell upon them. I ask you," Washington paused a moment, frowned and then continued, "if need be, could the United States become the arsenal of liberty again? I think not. The US automobile industry is in dire straits. There is scant production of steel, rubber and other materials necessary for the production of the planes, vessels, tanks and armaments that are required. The need to look to foreign countries for what we might need under those circumstances for those needs should be unacceptable to the United States and its people, but those considerations are rarely, if ever, mentioned. I cannot more strongly warn you and your countrymen to resist the loss of those factories and jobs and skills. It is vital that you retain the ability to produce what's necessary to defend the United States and its interests at home and abroad."

I nodded at President Washington. I had to agree with what he had just said. We certainly would be hard pressed to produce the weapons and other goods that we had produced to defeat Nazi Germany and Japan, but I knew that many people of my generation didn't think we ever would need to do so. We had the nuclear deterrent. I said, "We have a full supply of missiles and warheads and planes to deliver bombs, including nuclear bombs, anywhere in the world. Do you think we need trucks and tanks and a navy, when most of my contemporaries vow to never again send our young men and women into a ground war on foreign soil?"

"Situations could easily arise where we would need all of the more traditional means of waging a war, and I'm sure situations could occur where you and the people of your time would agree that the United States should intercede."

I didn't mean to be stubborn, but I persisted. "Could you give me an example of that kind of event?"

"Certainly." President Washington thought a moment, then nodded and said, "Assume that there is a large influx of people from Algeria and other parts of North Africa into France. Perhaps there was some real or imagined insult to the immigrant community already there, or to Mohammed or the Muslim religion by some member of the French government. That has happened in your time and out-of-control rioting followed for several days."

I nodded in agreement as I said, "I remembered reporting those stories only a short time ago."

Washington continued. "In any event, they come armed, and with the intention of joining with the immigrant population from North Africa already in France to overthrow the duly elected president of France and to seize power for themselves. They take control of Marseille and bring in even more armed fighters from the Islamic Fascist societies, together with small tanks, trucks, machine guns and similar non-nuclear weapons. The French police and army are unable to stop them and they occupy part of southern France and announce that it is a new Islamic Republic."

President Washington must somehow have noticed that I found it difficult to accept his assumption, but, before I could say anything, Washington said, "Please, do not think this is not possible. The French abandoned Algeria in 1962 because they were unable to resist those very same forces. I see the French no more able in your time than they were in 1962. Remember, that until that abandonment, Algeria was considered as much a part of France as Alaska is of the United States."

I knew that, but had forgotten it.

"Also assume that the President of France asks the UN and its neighbors for assistance. The UN condemns the attack but does nothing. The Germans and the British have their own minorities who side with the Islamic invaders and threaten their own insurrection if the German or British governments assist the French. The Germans and British then refuse to help France. That, too, is a not unlikely event. Appeasement has a long and sorry history in Europe. The French then turn to the United States. They ask for guns, trucks and tanks. They ask that the US navy blockade Marseille to prevent more Islamic fighters and armaments from entering France. Leave the question aside for now as to whether the United

States should come to their assistance and consider that you may not have the ability to help them if the current trend were to continue."

I asked. He answered. I had to admit that I was surprised that he changed my mind so quickly and easily about the possibility of our need to fight a conventional war. "Do you seriously think that Algeria would ever invade France?"

President Washington smiled. "France invaded Algeria. Don't the people of your time say that 'Turnabout is fair play,'?" Washington smiled, "It was Lincoln who coined that phrase while running for Congress." Washington turned serious again as he said, "I am very serious. Actually, it would not be the Algerian formal government that would invade France. I agree that is far fetched. In my example, it's the inhabitants of Algeria joined by other members of the Islamist Jihad movement who are urged to do so by the clerics who are a part of that government who would do the invading and fighting, and they certainly would do it, if they believe they could succeed, and perhaps they can. You can just as easily substitute Spain for France in the example I used, and the Balkans are another area the Islamic Fascists could choose to invade. I don't think the scenario is impossible at all. Much of those areas were once under Muslim control, and the restoration of that rule is a goal of the Islamic Fascists of your time. It may be unlikely at this moment, but what about ten or twenty years later in your time?"

I took a moment to consider Washington's example and then said, "As I think about what you just said, I think your example could easily become next year's headlines. Osama Bin Laden and his followers are looking for something to dwarf nine eleven. Seizing Marseille and southern France would do that. You said we would pass, at least temporarily, on a discussion of whether we should come to the assistance of the French. Can I ask you about that now?"

Washington nodded. "I would be inclined to come to their aid, provided it did not mean I had to decimate my forces or deplete my inventory of armaments and supplies. Unlike Europe, the United States had pursued a strategy of inclusion with its immigrants rather than one of exclusion. Economic factors and a greater degree of comfort and familiarity with one's former countrymen and other immigrant populations cause some de-facto isolation of immigrant communities in the United States, but it's an issue that the United States attempts to minimize. No similar effort was made in most of Europe. I should hope we could resist those of our citizens who wish to follow the European model and engage in appeasement, the ones who once said, 'better red than dead' during the Cold War."

"I'm a little surprised to hear you say that you think we should help the French. From my reading of your Farewell Address, I thought you were an isolationist."

"I was, and it was more sensible to be one when Europe was almost always involved in some war somewhere and we were barely able to keep our fledgling government functioning. The barrier of the ocean in an age of jet travel and instant communication is no longer the substantial barrier it once was. We are more able to help ourselves and others when it suits our interest to do so. However, not every dispute everywhere should become our concern. The particular example I posed does merit our attention. The risk of trouble in the US is substantially increased if the Islamic Fascists succeed in attacks like the one proposed. Spain would most likely be next, and then the Balkans, and most likely Greece and Italy. Eventually, all of Europe would be overrun and we would become increasingly isolated and would be a future target in their plan of world domination by their theocracy."

I frowned, a little confused by what was being said. "So, if I understand you correctly, you think we should send aid, but not our troops?"

"In my example, that was all that was sought."

I persisted. "That's right, but if they asked for troops, should we send them?"

Washington thought a moment, then said, "Probably not. They must prize their way of life and their liberty and freedom enough to fight for it themselves. If they are unwilling to fight for it, I see no reason why your president should send your men and women to do the fighting for them. If the United States indicates its willingness to do the fighting and dying, why should they? I have told you this once before and you had agreed with me. Shall I assume you still do?"

Washington had again managed to easily turn my thoughts back and forth. My first inclination was to do nothing if the UN refused to authorize resistance and call for a coalition of forces to assist the French, and that inclination was strengthened when he said Britain and Germany refused to help. When he explained the danger, it seemed to me that we couldn't allow France to fall to the Islamic Fascists under any circumstances and that we ought to send our troops in if asked to do so, and now, perhaps not. It's true. If we are willing to do the fighting and dying, why should anyone else? They have to want to be free badly enough to fight and die for it. I thought for a moment of Washington and his men taking on the British Empire. They had wanted freedom and liberty enough to walk away from all of the comforts of life and risk death and die for it. "You're right," I said, "but I'm sure they will want freedom badly enough to fight for it themselves."

"I'm not as sure of that as you are. People who have never experienced living without liberty, who have had it as a birthright, as have your countrymen in your time, or who have forgotten what it's like not to have it, do not always prize it sufficiently. Consider that the Europeans that most passionately prize freedom and liberty are the Europeans who most recently dwelled behind the Soviet Iron Curtain." Washington paused momentarily and then said, "We were meeting to discuss your economy and my major concern for you and the people of your time is that they recognize that it is in their best interest that they insist that the economy be able to produce what the nation needs to survive. That is the first obligation of government. Laws must be enacted with incentives and protections that guarantee that you retain the necessary industry to protect yourselves and, when appropriate, your friends and neighbors in the community of nations."

"Is there more to be said on this subject?" I asked.

"We've hardly begun, but I fear that is all we can manage for today. We shall meet here tomorrow morning as usual and we will talk further on the economy and defense of the nation."

11

President Washington was seated at our usual table sipping his tea when I arrived. For a moment or two, he seemed to disappear. I heard a female voice saying someone might soon be awake. I felt like something was poking at me, and I didn't like it. The voices and poking stopped and I was once again finishing breakfast with President Washington. After breakfast, Washington started the interview by saying, "When Alexander Hamilton spoke to you about energy issues, there was much more he wanted to say. I felt we had probably covered what we had to. Alex was dining with Churchill at that time; and, since Winston has been known to take offense rather easily, I decided to postpone the rest of the discussion and suggested that he return to his table." President Washington paused and looked at me a moment before continuing. "I'm sure you agree that we demonstrated that it is necessary to end our oil dependency and cease subsidizing our enemies for our very survival."

I nodded. "Absolutely," I said. "Nothing could be clearer."

President Washington nodded and smiled. "Good. Now, I want to continue our discussion of energy, but shift its focus from denying funds to our enemy to the defense of the nation, your economy and your liberty and freedom. Yesterday we spoke of the necessity of your retaining the means to produce the armaments necessary to protect the nation. That is also good for the economy and a strong economy is a needed weapon in the war against Islamic Fascism. Let me say it a little differently. It's my view that a strong economy is necessary, not only for the felicity of the people, but is also necessary for national defense and as an example to the world that demonstrates the superiority of our system that is based on liberty and freedom. All that requires a strong economy and a strong economy requires a reliable and inexpensive source of power, so they are all inter-related. The continuing increases in costs of oil make the production of good and services more expensive. It makes the cost of gasoline and shipments of goods and services more expensive. It makes it expensive to heat and cool your homes, to run elevators, to do the things you all take for granted in current society. In short, it threatens to destroy your economy."

Washington paused a moment to let what he said sink in. He continued. "The destruction of your economy could, in turn, result in the destruction of your system of government and could lead to the kind of chaos that often results in the overthrow of democratic forms of government in favor of a fascist or military government. A prime example from fairly recent history is the chaos in Germany in the late nineteen twenties and early thirties that led to the Nazi dictatorship. An educated and highly civilized society was willing to surrender a chaotic and inefficient democracy that failed to produce stable economic conditions in favor of a more orderly fascist dictatorship that took their freedom and liberty from them, because it promised better economic conditions. You are familiar with that situation, aren't you?"

I nodded that I was.

"Good." Washington nodded at me, furrowed his forehead in deep thought for a moment before continuing, and then said, "If I had to choose one technology to combat the energy crisis in the United States, it would be nuclear. It, of all the other methods, is the fastest, safest, least disruptive and cheapest of all the solutions. It can be fed into and add to the current distribution system and eventually replace all the fossil fuel facilities in the entire country. The engineering work to build and operate uranium fueled reactors has been done most notably in the United States, France and Germany. Despite what has been said about it by well-meaning hysterics, it is essentially very safe and cheap, and the disposal problems are not as bad as they are made out to be. It would be the quickest solution for the energy problem."

"I know you feel that way and at this point, I believe it too. However, despite what you have said, I think it's almost impossible to gain support for a nuclear energy solution."

"That's my main reason for supporting a change from uranium to thorium. As I said before, it's safer, doesn't have the waste disposal problems inherent in uranium and the wastes cannot easily be made into bombs, but the main reason is that it is relatively unknown and doesn't have the reputation that uranium does. Politicians in your time find it difficult if not impossible to ever admit they were wrong about anything. They call it 'flip-flopping' and that's apparently a very bad thing. I wonder if the people who thought the world was flat and those that said the sun revolved around the earth were reviled for 'flip-flopping' when they had to change their minds and admit they were wrong. Perhaps I'll ask them when I get a chance." Washington paused momentarily and then continued, "But in any event, it is probably easier, quicker and better to change to using thorium and doing the extra engineering work than trying to persuade a group of politicians that they were not infallible and had been wrong about uranium."

I knew there would be resistance, even to thorium. People would have trouble getting past the word nuclear. I asked, "Couldn't we do that with solar and wind?"

"At this time in your world, solar and wind cannot solve the problem. There is no technology that can provide the necessary storage facilities for the power that can be produced by those means to make it available where and when it's needed. When the sun is not shining and there is no wind, stored power becomes necessary. Where would you store the power to run a city inhabited by millions of people?" Washington frowned. "Solar and wind can be used on an individual basis, but unfortunately, they are not the answer to the real problem. They are at best ancillary to another system."

"If that's the case, why don't we forget about wind and solar and thermal and all the rest and concentrate on nuclear energy?"

"We could, but as I said, many may choose to use solar or wind energy at their home to avoid or reduce even that small expense, and we must consider the needs of small and isolated communities that might be better served by wind, solar or perhaps hydro power. For example, the small island economies like those of the American Virgin Islands and the other Caribbean islands. Some of the smaller Hawaiian Islands and other islands do not require the amounts of power that are generated from a nuclear facility and their more modest requirement may be more economically filled by a combination of solar and wind power that can be increased by turbines turned by the ebb and flow of the tides, if necessary. There are other small scattered communities in Africa and Asia that might also be best serviced in that manner. There are many places around the world that will not need the power that would be generated from a nuclear reactor." Washington paused a moment for a sip of tea. "The economists tell us that it is American consumer spending that supports the world economies, and consumers are best served by low prices for consumer goods. That should not be your main focus, even if it is true. People need to produce valuable goods and services for their own sense of accomplishment, and, more importantly, do something that will benefit others. The people of your time can do that. They can work on the technology required to produce solar energy. They can work on technologies to produce wind energy and turbines to be placed in the oceans and rivers without disturbing navigation or harming the environment. Their expertise in those technologies will produce great economic benefits for the people of the United States and strengthen their economy. Scientists and engineers are now studying the feasibility of their building a thorium powered reactor in India. Whoever first demonstrates that they have mastered that technology will have a profitable enterprise to conduct throughout the world. You have more experience with that technology than anyone else and you should not lose that advantage. After all, the first thorium fueled reactor in the world was built and operated in Pennsylvania almost fifty years ago."

Surprised by what I had just heard, it took me a minute to compose the questions I had to ask. "What happened to it? Was it a success, and, if it was, why didn't we build more of them?"

President Washington must have sensed that there were many more questions I wanted to ask. He smiled at me and said, "The reactor operated successfully for a number of years, but it didn't produce the kind of plutonium that the Defense Department wanted so it could make an inventory of nuclear bombs. The industry converted to uranium and that ended all efforts to use thorium for the production of electrical energy. Technological improvements over the years will allow lowered costs and greater efficiency, but the experience the country has had should be to its advantage."

Washington paused a moment to sip his tea thoughtfully. "Another thing you and your countrymen should also always remember is that even though thorium is plentiful in the United States and elsewhere, eventually, it too may become in short supply, or advances in solar energy technology or other technologies may make some other source of energy better than thorium. The people of the United States in your time should acquire the expertise in thorium and all those technologies which will become necessary to meet the basic energy needs for an increasing world population that requires increasing amounts of energy on a per capita basis. What do you think will happen when the enormous populations of China and India acquire the means to themselves enjoy the benefits of modern society? If you and they continue to rely on fossil fuels, the supply will dissipate all the sooner, the atmosphere will be even more polluted and you will all suffer." After another sip of his tea, Washington said, "You and the people of your time in the United States have a wonderful economic opportunity that can enhance your own lives by leading the world in all those technologies. Don't squander it with indecision and political ineptitude. Take advantage of it."

We sat quietly for a moment. I thought that perhaps Washington had said all that he wanted to say about energy.

Washington looked at me closely for a moment and then said, "I didn't think we would have time to get to this issue, but I believe we have enough time to at least give it some consideration." He paused a moment, seeming to gather his thoughts. "I want you to consider another one of the problems of your time that is infrequently mentioned that can only get worse. Like energy, it is a necessary ingredient of life, even more so."

My curiosity could not be restrained. "What problem is that?"

"It is the shortage of water, water to drink and water to irrigate your crops so you can produce the food that is needed to sustain life on the planet." Washington paused a moment to let what he had just said sink in. "There are shortages existing or beginning everywhere. In the United States, water shortages in the city of Atlanta recently made the headlines in your newspapers. The southwestern United States has chronic difficulties. And those problems are like nothing compared to the problems in Darfur and other places in Africa. The North African desert moves further and further to the south every decade. The population of the planet is increasing enormously, and as medical achievements lengthen life-spans, the demand for food and water will outstrip their availability in more and more places. Many of your political leaders at least recognize that there is an energy problem and talk about it, very few seem to understand that water availability is another problem and you hear almost nothing about it. And if that doesn't worry you about the near future of your planet, consider the longer range problem about the air you breathe. You hear from the environmental lobbyists about air pollution, but you hear nothing about the fact that if the forests and plants disappear, so will their ability to provide the oxygen that you need. Perhaps, if nothing is done, that will become a crisis after another century or two."

President Washington had paused a moment. There was obviously more to be said, but I couldn't imagine what. "You have a solution for those problems, I hope?"

Washington smiled. "Unlike with the health care problem, this time I believe I do. So much of the planet is water that the problem can be dealt with. Cheap power from nuclear energy can relieve drought and water shortage problems by supplying the energy required to maintain desalination plants. With sea water desalination plants energized by cheap electrical power, drinking water can be supplied to those that need it. Deserts can be made to bloom and produce the food necessary to feed the starving and oxygen for the planet. Advances in technology can produce exciting opportunities for economic advancement and the improvement of lives around the world. The people of the United States should be in the vanguard of those opportunities." Washington seemed more animated as he continued talking. "The future can be very bright. For now, it seems to me that thorium fueled reactors producing cheap electric power is where you should be going. I mentioned in passing research on fusion energy taking place in Provence. That may be the technology of the next century. The future is filled with possibilities. The United States and its people should lead the way and not be plagued with political and bureaucratic red tape that frustrates accomplishing worthwhile changes as it now is."

I had not previously heard President Washington speak so passionately about anything. He seemed excited and yet sad. "I hope we do, I said." I paused a moment. President Washington must have noticed the frown on my face I couldn't control.

Washington said, "Do not be pessimistic," as he forced a smile. "The resolve we spoke of before is what's needed. A resolve to solve the energy problems and a resolve by the people of the country to change the confrontational manner of viewing what must be done. There is no Republican way and no Democrat way. There should only be an American way. It's the same issue I warned about in my Farewell Address, that TR spoke of in expressing his views on immigration." Washington smiled and said, "I could go on in this vein, but it would be redundant, and we must talk about automobiles and planes. No discussion of energy needs can be complete without discussing those major users of energy."

"I came away from our prior discussions thinking that you wanted us to develop ethanol from sugar as a fuel source."

"Quite right. As I said before, the interests promoted by certain members of Congress for using corn will only drive up food prices and will add to the burdens of your countrymen. It's another example of the selfish partisanship that rules the discourse of this time. Sugar is a cheaper, more efficient and far better source, but I don't want to repeat what we have already dealt with. Let's move on."

I was still stuck on ethanol. I had my reservations about the willingness of the people of the United States to turn to nuclear power plants, even if thorium was as good a solution as I was told. Ethanol was something we could do without running into political problems. I asked, "Could enough ethanol be produced from sugar crops to run the automobiles of the world?"

Washington shrugged. "I really don't know, but just think about how much sugar cane ethanol could be produced if the deserts of the southwestern United States were irrigated with desalinated water and if the deserts of Africa were similarly irrigated."

I thought about it for a moment and said, "What a different looking world we could have if we could do that." What I thought, but kept to myself, was the realization that nuclear energy power plants, thorium or uranium, had to become a reality.

President Washington continued. "There is an opportunity for the American automobile industry to rise like a phoenix from the funeral pyre in which it placed itself with inefficient automobiles that were technologically behind the advances made by its competitors. As I said before, they are a necessity for our national defense and deserve some help if they are willing to produce what they should for the current times. Perhaps the ultimate answer may be electric automobiles that can be charged with cheap thorium produced electricity. That remains to be seen. As I understand it, there are times when more acceleration is needed than can be obtained from the kind of electric motors current technology knows how to produce. That is a problem that may be solved in due course, but for now, in your time, and until the problem is solved, ethanol powered ancillary engines should be used for that purpose instead of gasoline engines, or perhaps some kind of bio-diesel powered engine may be used by some. Henry Ford and George Washington Carver experimented with that type of fuel about eighty years ago. Until the new nuclear facilities are all up and running, ethanol or some other technology should provide the main fuel for your automobiles and trucks. That can be done quickly and inexpensively."

"If automobiles are electric powered, except for any assist provided by ancillary ethanol or bio-diesel powered engines, ethanol and bio-diesel demand will decline."

Washington nodded. "I would expect that to happen."

"Assume ethanol is the power source until the electric car takes over." President Washington nodded for me to continue. I said, "I wonder if sugar growers and ethanol providers will be willing to make the investment necessary to produce substantial amounts of ethanol, if the handwriting is on the wall that ethanol power will be substantially phased out."

"If the ethanol requirements of the auto industry are reduced, ethanol production could become the main source of fuel for ships at sea, for military use and wherever recharging facilities may not be readily available. Ethanol powered generators would be useful additions in areas where power failures occur. I suspect that there will be strong demand for ethanol for a very long time as there is no one answer to the entire energy problem. However, the world changes and new technologies replace old ones. Whale oil was once a principal source of fuel for lighting. Businesses grow and decline. As Titus Lucretius Carus, the Roman Epicurean poet said, 'De rerum natura'."

I looked at President Washington. It was obvious that I had no idea what he had just said.

"Sorry about that. Jefferson favored the Epicurean philosophers and persuaded me to study them as well. It refers to the nature of things, and, in the present context, sums up the way businesses and technologies come forward and are eventually replaced."

Washington refilled his tea cup. He smiled before continuing and saying, "We knew that before we embarked on our journey in self-government." Turning serious again, he said, "I can only hope that providing a method of amending the Constitution will enable future generations of Americans to preserve all that is basic and good in our experiment in self-governance and save it from history's scrap heap."

"That will never happen," I said. As I spoke those words, President Washington disappeared. I could dimly hear him say, as if he were far away, "Remember what we spoke about." The next minute I heard that female voice again.

I focused my eyes. I was in a room with light colored walls. I couldn't see the eighteenth green. There was that female sounding voice again. I looked at where the voice was coming from. Yes, it was a woman. She was dressed all in white. I didn't know who she was. I didn't know where I was. I looked out the window. It looked like there was a field out there, and children, girls, were on that field kicking a ball. I again looked around the room I was in. It looked and smelled like a hospital. I looked at the woman standing over me. She was staring into my eyes as I heard her say, "He's awake. All his vitals are good." The woman smiled at me and said, "Welcome back, sweetie. Don't know where you been, but you were there for quite a while."

THE END

Addenda

THE CONSTITUTION OF THE UNITED STATES

We the People of the United States, in Order to form a more perfect Union, establish Justice, insure domestic Tranquility, provide for the common defence, promote the general Welfare, and secure the Blessings of Liberty to ourselves and our Posterity, do ordain and establish this Constitution for the United States of America.

Article. I.

Section 1—All legislative Powers herein granted shall be vested in a Congress of the United States, which shall consist of a Senate and House of Representatives.

Section 2—The House of Representatives shall be composed of Members chosen every second Year by the People of the several States, and the Electors in each State shall have the Qualifications requisite for Electors of the most numerous Branch of the State Legislature.

No Person shall be a Representative who shall not have attained to the Age of twenty five Years, and been seven Years a Citizen of the United States, and who shall not, when elected, be an Inhabitant of that State in which he shall be chosen.

(Representatives and direct Taxes shall be apportioned among the several States which may be included within this Union, according to their respective Numbers, which shall be determined by adding to the whole Number of free Persons, including those bound to Service for a Term of Years, and excluding Indians not taxed, three fifths of all other Persons.) (The previous sentence in italics was modified by the 14th Amendment, section 2.) The actual Enumeration shall be made within three Years after the first Meeting of the Congress of the United States, and within every subsequent Term of ten Years, in such Manner as they shall by Law direct.

The Number of Representatives shall not exceed one for every thirty Thousand, but each State shall have at Least one Representative; and until such enumeration shall be made, the State of New Hampshire shall be entitled to chuse three, Massachusetts eight, Rhode Island and Providence Plantations one, Connecticut five, New York six, New Jersey four, Pennsylvania eight, Delaware one, Maryland six, Virginia ten, North Carolina five, South Carolina five and Georgia three.

When vacancies happen in the Representation from any State, the Executive Authority thereof shall issue Writs of Election to fill such Vacancies.

The House of Representatives shall chuse their Speaker and other Officers; and shall have the sole Power of Impeachment.

Section 3—The Senate The Senate of the United States shall be composed of two Senators from each State, *(chosen by the Legislature thereof,)* (The preceding words in italics were superseded by 17th Amendment, section 1.) for six Years; and each Senator shall have one Vote.

Immediately after they shall be assembled in Consequence of the first Election, they shall be divided as equally as may be into three Classes. The Seats of the Senators of the first Class shall be vacated at the Expiration of the second Year, of the second Class at the Expiration of the fourth Year, and of the third Class at the Expiration of the sixth Year, so that one third may be chosen every second Year; *(and if Vacancies happen by Resignation, or otherwise, during the Recess of the Legislature of any State, the Executive thereof may make temporary Appointments until the next Meeting of the Legislature, which shall then fill such Vacancies.)* (The preceding words in italics were superseded by the 17th Amendment, section 2.)

No person shall be a Senator who shall not have attained to the Age of thirty Years, and been nine Years a Citizen of the United States, and who shall not, when elected, be an Inhabitant of that State for which he shall be chosen.

The Vice President of the United States shall be President of the Senate, but shall have no Vote, unless they be equally divided.

The Senate shall chuse their other Officers, and also a President pro tempore, in the absence of the Vice President, or when he shall exercise the Office of President of the United States.

The Senate shall have the sole Power to try all Impeachments. When sitting for that Purpose, they shall be on Oath or Affirmation. When the President of the United States is tried, the Chief Justice shall preside: And no Person shall be convicted without the Concurrence of two thirds of the Members present.

Judgment in Cases of Impeachment shall not extend further than to removal from Office, and disqualification to hold and enjoy any Office of honor, Trust or Profit under the United States: but the Party convicted shall nevertheless be liable and subject to Indictment, Trial, Judgment and Punishment, according to Law.

Section 4—Elections, Meetings The Times, Places and Manner of holding Elections for Senators and Representatives, shall be prescribed in each State by the Legislature thereof; but the Congress may at any time by Law make or alter such Regulations, except as to the Place of Chusing Senators.

The Congress shall assemble at least once in every Year, and such Meeting shall *(be on the first Monday in December,)* (The preceding words in italics were superseded by the 20th Amendment, section 2.) unless they shall by Law appoint a different Day.

Section 5—Membership, Rules, Journals, Adjournment Each House shall be the Judge of the Elections, Returns and Qualifications of its own Members, and a Majority of each shall constitute a Quorum to do Business; but a smaller number may adjourn from day to day, and may be authorized to compel the Attendance of absent Members, in such Manner, and under such Penalties as each House may provide.

Each House may determine the Rules of its Proceedings, punish its Members for disorderly Behavior, and, with the Concurrence of two-thirds, expel a Member.

Each House shall keep a Journal of its Proceedings, and from time to time publish the same, excepting such Parts as may in their Judgment require Secrecy; and the Yeas and Nays of the Members of either House on any question shall, at the Desire of one fifth of those Present, be entered on the Journal.

Neither House, during the Session of Congress, shall, without the Consent of the other, adjourn for more than three days, nor to any other Place than that in which the two Houses shall be sitting.

Section 6—Compensation *(The Senators and Representatives shall receive a Compensation for their Services, to be ascertained by Law, and paid out of the Treasury of the United States.)* (The preceding words in italics were modified by the 27th Amendment.) They shall in all Cases, except Treason, Felony and Breach of the Peace, be privileged from Arrest during their Attendance at the Session of their respective Houses, and in going to and returning from the same; and for any Speech or Debate in either House, they shall not be questioned in any other Place.

No Senator or Representative shall, during the Time for which he was elected, be appointed to any civil Office under the Authority of the United States which shall have been created, or the Emoluments whereof shall have been increased during such time; and no Person holding any Office under the United States, shall be a Member of either House during his Continuance in Office.

Section 7—Revenue Bills, Legislative Process, Presidential Veto All bills for raising Revenue shall originate in the House of Representatives; but the Senate may propose or concur with Amendments as on other Bills.

Every Bill which shall have passed the House of Representatives and the Senate, shall, before it become a Law, be presented to the President of the United States; If he approve he shall sign it, but if not he shall return it, with his Objections to that House in which it shall have originated, who shall enter the Objections at large on their Journal, and proceed to reconsider it. If after such Reconsideration two thirds of that House shall agree to pass the Bill, it shall be sent, together with the Objections, to the other House, by which it shall likewise be reconsidered, and if approved by two thirds of that House, it shall become a Law. But in all such Cases the Votes of both Houses shall be determined by Yeas and Nays, and the Names of the Persons voting for and against the Bill shall be entered on the Journal of each House respectively. If any Bill shall not be returned by the President within ten Days (Sundays excepted) after it shall have been presented to him, the Same shall be a Law, in like Manner as if he had signed it, unless the Congress by their Adjournment prevent its Return, in which Case it shall not be a Law.

Every Order, Resolution, or Vote to which the Concurrence of the Senate and House of Representatives may be necessary (except on a question of Adjournment) shall be presented to the President of the United States; and before the Same shall take Effect, shall be approved by him, or being disapproved by him, shall be repassed by two thirds of the Senate and House of Representatives, according to the Rules and Limitations prescribed in the Case of a Bill.

Section 8—Powers of Congress The Congress shall have Power To lay and collect Taxes, Duties, Imposts and Excises, to pay the Debts and provide for the common Defence and general Welfare of the United States; but all Duties, Imposts and Excises shall be uniform throughout the United States;

To borrow money on the credit of the United States;

To regulate Commerce with foreign Nations, and among the several States, and with the Indian Tribes;

To establish an uniform Rule of Naturalization, and uniform Laws on the subject of Bankruptcies throughout the United States;

To coin Money, regulate the Value thereof, and of foreign Coin, and fix the Standard of Weights and Measures;

To provide for the Punishment of counterfeiting the Securities and current Coin of the United States;

To establish Post Offices and Post Roads;

To promote the Progress of Science and useful Arts, by securing for limited Times to Authors and Inventors the exclusive Right to their respective Writings and Discoveries;

To constitute Tribunals inferior to the supreme Court;

To define and punish Piracies and Felonies committed on the high Seas, and Offenses against the Law of Nations;

To declare War, grant Letters of Marque and Reprisal, and make Rules concerning Captures on Land and Water;

To raise and support Armies, but no Appropriation of Money to that Use shall be for a longer Term than two Years;

To provide and maintain a Navy;

To make Rules for the Government and Regulation of the land and naval Forces;

To provide for calling forth the Militia to execute the Laws of the Union, suppress Insurrections and repel Invasions;

To provide for organizing, arming, and disciplining the Militia, and for governing such Part of them as may be employed in the Service of the United States, reserving to the States respectively, the Appointment of the Officers, and the Authority of training the Militia according to the discipline prescribed by Congress;

To exercise exclusive Legislation in all Cases whatsoever, over such District (not exceeding ten Miles square) as may, by Cession of particular States, and the acceptance of Congress, become the Seat of the Government of the United States, and to exercise like Authority over all Places purchased by the Consent of the Legislature of the State in which the Same shall be, for the Erection of Forts, Magazines, Arsenals, dock-Yards, and other needful Buildings; And

To make all Laws which shall be necessary and proper for carrying into Execution the foregoing Powers, and all other Powers vested by this Constitution in the Government of the United States, or in any Department or Officer thereof.

Section 9—Limits on Congress The Migration or Importation of such Persons as any of the States now existing shall think proper to admit, shall not be prohibited by the Congress prior to the Year one thousand eight hundred and eight, but a tax or duty may be imposed on such Importation, not exceeding ten dollars for each Person.

The privilege of the Writ of Habeas Corpus shall not be suspended, unless when in Cases of Rebellion or Invasion the public Safety may require it.

No Bill of Attainder or ex post facto Law shall be passed.

(No capitation, or other direct, Tax shall be laid, unless in Proportion to the Census or Enumeration herein before directed to be taken.) (Section in italics modified by the 16th Amendment.)

No Tax or Duty shall be laid on Articles exported from any State.

No Preference shall be given by any Regulation of Commerce or Revenue to the Ports of one State over those of another: nor shall Vessels bound to, or from, one State, be obliged to enter, clear, or pay Duties in another.

No Money shall be drawn from the Treasury, but in Consequence of Appropriations made by Law; and a regular Statement and Account of the Receipts and Expenditures of all public Money shall be published from time to time.

No Title of Nobility shall be granted by the United States: And no Person holding any Office of Profit or Trust under them, shall, without the Consent of the Congress, accept of any present, Emolument, Office, or Title, of any kind whatever, from any King, Prince or foreign State.

Section 10—Powers prohibited of States No State shall enter into any Treaty, Alliance, or Confederation; grant Letters of Marque and Reprisal; coin Money; emit Bills of Credit; make any Thing but gold and silver Coin a Tender in Payment of Debts; pass any Bill of Attainder, ex post facto Law, or Law impairing the Obligation of Contracts, or grant any Title of Nobility.

No State shall, without the Consent of the Congress, lay any Imposts or Duties on Imports or Exports, except what may be absolutely necessary for executing it's inspection Laws: and the net Produce of all Duties and Imposts, laid by any State on Imports or Exports, shall be for the Use of the Treasury of the United States; and all such Laws shall be subject to the Revision and Controul of the Congress.

No State shall, without the Consent of Congress, lay any duty of Tonnage, keep Troops, or Ships of War in time of Peace, enter into any Agreement or Compact with another State, or with a foreign Power, or engage in War, unless actually invaded, or in such imminent Danger as will not admit of delay.

Article. II.—The Executive Branch

Section 1—The President The executive Power shall be vested in a President of the United States of America. He shall hold his Office during the Term of four Years, and, together with the Vice-President chosen for the same Term, be elected, as follows:

Each State shall appoint, in such Manner as the Legislature thereof may direct, a Number of Electors, equal to the whole Number of Senators and Representatives to which the State may be entitled in the Congress: but no Senator or Representative, or Person holding an Office of Trust or Profit under the United States, shall be appointed an Elector.

(The Electors shall meet in their respective States, and vote by Ballot for two persons, of whom one at least shall not lie an Inhabitant of the same State with themselves. And they shall make a List of all the Persons voted for, and of the Number of Votes for each; which List they shall sign and certify, and transmit sealed to the Seat of the Government of the United States, directed to the President of the Senate. The President of the Senate shall, in the Presence of the Senate and House of Representatives, open all the Certificates, and the Votes shall then be counted. The Person having the greatest Number of Votes shall be the President, if such Number be a Majority of the whole Number of Electors appointed; and if there be more than one who have such Majority, and have an equal Number of Votes, then the House of Representatives shall immediately chuse by Ballot one of them for President; and if no Person have a Majority, then from the five highest on the List the said House shall in like Manner chuse the President. But in chusing the President, the Votes shall be taken by States, the Representation from each State having one Vote; a quorum for this Purpose shall consist of a Member or Members from two-thirds of the States, and a Majority of all the States shall be necessary to a Choice. In every Case, after the Choice of the President, the Person having the greatest Number of Votes of the Electors shall be the Vice President. But if there should remain two or more who have equal Votes, the Senate shall chuse from them by Ballot the Vice-President.) (This clause in italics was superseded by the 12th Amendment.)

The Congress may determine the Time of chusing the Electors, and the Day on which they shall give their Votes; which Day shall be the same throughout the United States.

No person except a natural born Citizen, or a Citizen of the United States, at the time of the Adoption of this Constitution, shall be eligible to the Office of President; neither shall any Person be eligible to that Office who shall not have attained to the Age of thirty-five Years, and been fourteen Years a Resident within the United States.

(In Case of the Removal of the President from Office, or of his Death, Resignation, or Inability to discharge the Powers and Duties of the said Office, the same shall devolve on the Vice President, and the Congress may by Law provide for the Case of Removal, Death, Resignation or Inability, both of the President and Vice President, declaring what Officer shall then act as President, and such Officer shall act accordingly, until the Disability be removed, or a President shall be elected.) (This clause in italics has been modified by the 20th and 25th Amendments.)

The President shall, at stated Times, receive for his Services, a Compensation, which shall neither be increased nor diminished during the Period for which he shall have been elected, and he shall not receive within that Period any other Emolument from the United States, or any of them.

Before he enter on the Execution of his Office, he shall take the following Oath or Affirmation:

"I do solemnly swear (or affirm) that I will faithfully execute the Office of President of the United States, and will to the best of my Ability, preserve, protect and defend the Constitution of the United States."

Section 2—Civilian Power over Military, Cabinet, Pardon Power, Appointments The President shall be Commander in Chief of the Army and Navy of the United States, and of the Militia of the several States, when called into the actual Service of the United States; he may require the Opinion, in writing, of the principal Officer in each of the executive Departments, upon any subject relating to the Duties of their respective Offices, and he shall have Power to Grant Reprieves and Pardons for Offenses against the United States, except in Cases of Impeachment.

He shall have Power, by and with the Advice and Consent of the Senate, to make Treaties, provided two thirds of the Senators present concur; and he shall nominate, and by and with the Advice and Consent of the Senate, shall appoint Ambassadors, other public Ministers and Consuls, Judges of the supreme Court, and all other Officers of the United States, whose Appointments are not herein otherwise provided for, and which shall be established by Law: but the Congress may by Law vest the Appointment of such inferior Officers, as they think proper, in the President alone, in the Courts of Law, or in the Heads of Departments.

The President shall have Power to fill up all Vacancies that may happen during the Recess of the Senate, by granting Commissions which shall expire at the End of their next Session.

Section 3—State of the Union, Convening Congress He shall from time to time give to the Congress Information of the State of the Union, and recommend to their Consideration such Measures as he shall judge necessary and expedient; he may, on extraordinary Occasions, convene both Houses, or either of them, and in Case of Disagreement between them, with Respect to the Time of Adjournment, he may adjourn them to such Time as he shall think proper; he shall receive Ambassadors and other public Ministers; he shall take Care that the Laws be faithfully executed, and shall Commission all the Officers of the United States.

Section 4—Disqualification The President, Vice President and all civil Officers of the United States, shall be removed from Office on Impeachment for, and Conviction of, Treason, Bribery, or other high Crimes and Misdemeanors.

Article III.—The Judicial Branch

Section 1—Judicial powers The judicial Power of the United States, shall be vested in one supreme Court, and in such inferior Courts as the Congress may from time to time ordain and establish. The Judges, both of the supreme and inferior Courts, shall hold their Offices during good Behavior, and shall, at stated Times, receive for their Services a Compensation which shall not be diminished during their Continuance in Office.

Section 2—Trial by Jury, Original Jurisdiction, Jury Trials *(The judicial Power shall extend to all Cases, in Law and Equity, arising under this Constitution, the Laws of the United States, and Treaties made, or which shall be made, under their Authority; to all Cases affecting Ambassadors, other public Ministers and Con-*

suls; to all Cases of admiralty and maritime Jurisdiction; to Controversies to which the United States shall be a Party; to Controversies between two or more States; between a State and Citizens of another State; between Citizens of different States; between Citizens of the same State claiming Lands under Grants of different States, and between a State, or the Citizens thereof, and foreign States, Citizens or Subjects.) (This section in italics is modified by the 11th Amendment.)

In all Cases affecting Ambassadors, other public Ministers and Consuls, and those in which a State shall be Party, the supreme Court shall have original Jurisdiction. In all the other Cases before mentioned, the supreme Court shall have appellate Jurisdiction, both as to Law and Fact, with such Exceptions, and under such Regulations as the Congress shall make.

The Trial of all Crimes, except in Cases of Impeachment, shall be by Jury; and such Trial shall be held in the State where the said Crimes shall have been committed; but when not committed within any State, the Trial shall be at such Place or Places as the Congress may by Law have directed.

Section 3—Treason Treason against the United States, shall consist only in levying War against them, or in adhering to their Enemies, giving them Aid and Comfort. No Person shall be convicted of Treason unless on the Testimony of two Witnesses to the same overt Act, or on Confession in open Court.

The Congress shall have power to declare the Punishment of Treason, but no Attainder of Treason shall work Corruption of Blood, or Forfeiture except during the Life of the Person attainted.

Article. IV.—The States

Section 1—Each State to Honor all others Full Faith and Credit shall be given in each State to the public Acts, Records, and judicial Proceedings of every other State. And the Congress may by general Laws prescribe the Manner in which such Acts, Records and Proceedings shall be proved, and the Effect thereof.

Section 2—State citizens, Extradition The Citizens of each State shall be entitled to all Privileges and Immunities of Citizens in the several States.

A Person charged in any State with Treason, Felony, or other Crime, who shall flee from Justice, and be found in another State, shall on demand of the executive Authority of the State from which he fled, be delivered up, to be removed to the State having Jurisdiction of the Crime.

(No Person held to Service or Labour in one State, under the Laws thereof, escaping into another, shall, in Consequence of any Law or Regulation therein, be discharged from such Service or Labour, But shall be delivered up on Claim of the Party to whom such Service or Labour may be due.) (This clause in italics is superseded by the 13th Amendment.)

Section 3—New States New States may be admitted by the Congress into this Union; but no new States shall be formed or erected within the Jurisdiction of any other State; nor any State be formed by the Junction of two or more States, or parts of States, without the Consent of the Legislatures of the States concerned as well as of the Congress.

The Congress shall have Power to dispose of and make all needful Rules and Regulations respecting the Territory or other Property belonging to the United States; and nothing in this Constitution shall be so construed as to Prejudice any Claims of the United States, or of any particular State.

Section 4—Republican government The United States shall guarantee to every State in this Union a Republican Form of Government, and shall protect each of them against Invasion; and on Application of the Legislature, or of the Executive (when the Legislature cannot be convened) against domestic Violence.

Article. V.—Amendment

The Congress, whenever two thirds of both Houses shall deem it necessary, shall propose Amendments to this Constitution, or, on the Application of the Legislatures of two thirds of the several States, shall call a Convention for proposing Amendments, which, in either Case, shall be valid to all Intents and Purposes, as part of this Constitution, when ratified by the Legislatures of three fourths of the several States, or by Conventions in three fourths thereof, as the one or the other Mode of Ratification may be proposed by the Congress; Provided that no Amendment which may be made prior to the Year One thousand eight hundred and eight shall in any Manner affect the first and fourth Clauses in the Ninth

Section of the first Article; and that no State, without its Consent, shall be deprived of its equal Suffrage in the Senate.

Article. VI.—Debts, Supremacy, Oaths

All Debts contracted and Engagements entered into, before the Adoption of this Constitution, shall be as valid against the United States under this Constitution, as under the Confederation.

This Constitution, and the Laws of the United States which shall be made in Pursuance thereof; and all Treaties made, or which shall be made, under the Authority of the United States, shall be the supreme Law of the Land; and the Judges in every State shall be bound thereby, any Thing in the Constitution or Laws of any State to the Contrary notwithstanding.

The Senators and Representatives before mentioned, and the Members of the several State Legislatures, and all executive and judicial Officers, both of the United States and of the several States, shall be bound by Oath or Affirmation, to support this Constitution; but no religious Test shall ever be required as a Qualification to any Office or public Trust under the United States.

Article. VII.—Ratification *Documents*

The Ratification of the Conventions of nine States, shall be sufficient for the Establishment of this Constitution between the States so ratifying the Same.

Done in Convention by the Unanimous Consent of the States present the Seventeenth Day of September in the Year of our Lord one thousand seven hundred and Eighty seven and of the Independence of the United States of America the Twelfth. In Witness whereof We have hereunto subscribed our Names.

Go Washington—President and deputy from Virginia

New Hampshire—John Langdon, Nicholas Gilman

Massachusetts—Nathaniel Gorham, Rufus King

Connecticut—Wm Saml Johnson, Roger Sherman

New York—Alexander Hamilton

New Jersey—Wil Livingston, David Brearley, Wm Paterson, Jona. Dayton

Pensylvania—B Franklin, Thomas Mifflin, Robt Morris, Geo. Clymer, Thos FitzSimons, Jared Ingersoll, James Wilson, Gouv Morris

Delaware—Geo. Read, Gunning Bedford jun, John Dickinson, Richard Bassett, Jaco. Broom

Maryland—James McHenry, Dan of St Tho Jenifer, Danl Carroll

Virginia—John Blair, James Madison Jr.

North Carolina—Wm Blount, Richd Dobbs Spaight, Hu Williamson

South Carolina—J. Rutledge, Charles Cotesworth Pinckney, Charles Pinckney, Pierce Butler

Georgia—William Few, Abr Baldwin

Attest: William Jackson, Secretary

THE AMENDMENTS

The following are the Amendments to the Constitution. The first ten Amendments collectively are commonly known as the Bill of Rights.

Amendment 1—Freedom of Religion, Press, Expression. Ratified 12/15/1791.

Congress shall make no law respecting an establishment of religion, or prohibiting the free exercise thereof; or abridging the freedom of speech, or of the press; or the right of the people peaceably to assemble, and to petition the Government for a redress of grievances.

Amendment 2—Right to Bear Arms. Ratified 12/15/1791.

A well regulated Militia, being necessary to the security of a free State, the right of the people to keep and bear Arms, shall not be infringed.

Amendment 3—Quartering of Soldiers. Ratified 12/15/1791.

No Soldier shall, in time of peace be quartered in any house, without the consent of the Owner, nor in time of war, but in a manner to be prescribed by law.

Amendment 4—Search and Seizure. Ratified 12/15/1791.

The right of the people to be secure in their persons, houses, papers, and effects, against unreasonable searches and seizures, shall not be violated, and no Warrants shall issue, but upon probable cause, supported by Oath or affirmation, and particularly describing the place to be searched, and the persons or things to be seized.

Amendment 5—Trial and Punishment, Compensation for Takings. Ratified 12/15/1791.

No person shall be held to answer for a capital, or otherwise infamous crime, unless on a presentment or indictment of a Grand Jury, except in cases arising in the land or naval forces, or in the Militia, when in actual service in time of War or public danger; nor shall any person be subject for the same offense to be twice put in jeopardy of life or limb; nor shall be compelled in any criminal case to be a witness against himself, nor be deprived of life, liberty, or property, without due process of law; nor shall private property be taken for public use, without just compensation.

Amendment 6—Right to Speedy Trial, Confrontation of Witnesses. Ratified 12/15/1791.

In all criminal prosecutions, the accused shall enjoy the right to a speedy and public trial, by an impartial jury of the State and district wherein the crime shall have been committed, which district shall have been previously ascertained by law, and to be informed of the nature and cause of the accusation; to be confronted with the witnesses against him; to have compulsory process for obtaining witnesses in his favor, and to have the Assistance of Counsel for his defence.

Amendment 7—Trial by Jury in Civil Cases. Ratified 12/15/1791.

In Suits at common law, where the value in controversy shall exceed twenty dollars, the right of trial by jury shall be preserved, and no fact tried by a jury, shall be otherwise re-examined in any Court of the United States, than according to the rules of the common law.

Amendment 8—Cruel and Unusual Punishment. Ratified 12/15/1791.

Excessive bail shall not be required, nor excessive fines imposed, nor cruel and unusual punishments inflicted.

Amendment 9—Construction of Constitution. Ratified 12/15/1791.

The enumeration in the Constitution, of certain rights, shall not be construed to deny or disparage others retained by the people.

Amendment 10—Powers of the States and People. Ratified 12/15/1791.

The powers not delegated to the United States by the Constitution, nor prohibited by it to the States, are reserved to the States respectively, or to the people.

Amendment 11—Judicial Limits. Ratified 2/7/1795.

The Judicial power of the United States shall not be construed to extend to any suit in law or equity, commenced or prosecuted against one of the United States by Citizens of another State, or by Citizens or Subjects of any Foreign State.

Amendment 12—Choosing the President, Vice-President. Ratified 6/15/1804.

The Electors shall meet in their respective states, and vote by ballot for President and Vice-President, one of whom, at least, shall not be an inhabitant of the same state with themselves; they shall name in their ballots the person voted for as President, and in distinct ballots the person voted for as Vice-President, and they shall make distinct lists of all persons voted for as President, and of all persons voted for as Vice-President and of the number of votes for each, which lists they shall sign and certify, and transmit sealed to the seat of the government of the United States, directed to the President of the Senate;

The President of the Senate shall, in the presence of the Senate and House of Representatives, open all the certificates and the votes shall then be counted;

The person having the greatest Number of votes for President, shall be the President, if such number be a majority of the whole number of Electors appointed; and if no person have such majority, then from the persons having the highest numbers not exceeding three on the list of those voted for as President, the House of Representatives shall choose immediately, by ballot, the President. But in choosing the President, the votes shall be taken by states, the representation from each state having one vote; a quorum for this purpose shall consist of a member or members from two-thirds of the states, and a majority of all the states shall be necessary to a choice. And if the House of Representatives shall not choose a President whenever the right of choice shall devolve upon them, before the fourth day of March next following, then the Vice-President shall act as President, as in the case of the death or other constitutional disability of the President.

The person having the greatest number of votes as Vice-President, shall be the Vice-President, if such number be a majority of the whole number of Electors appointed, and if no person have a majority, then from the two highest numbers on the list, the Senate shall choose the Vice-President; a quorum for the purpose shall consist of two-thirds of the whole number of Senators, and a majority of the whole number shall be necessary to a choice. But no person constitutionally ineligible to the office of President shall be eligible to that of Vice-President of the United States.

Amendment 13—Slavery Abolished. Ratified 12/6/1865.

1. Neither slavery nor involuntary servitude, except as a punishment for crime whereof the party shall have been duly convicted, shall exist within the United States, or any place subject to their jurisdiction.

2. Congress shall have power to enforce this article by appropriate legislation.

Amendment 14—Citizenship Rights. Ratified 7/9/1868.

1. All persons born or naturalized in the United States, and subject to the jurisdiction thereof, are citizens of the United States and of the State wherein they reside. No State shall make or enforce any law which shall abridge the privileges or immunities of citizens of the United States; nor shall any State deprive any person of life, liberty, or property, without due process of law; nor deny to any person within its jurisdiction the equal protection of the laws.

2. Representatives shall be apportioned among the several States according to their respective numbers, counting the whole number of persons in each State, excluding Indians not taxed. But when the right to vote at any election for the choice of electors for President and Vice-President of the United States, Representatives in Congress, the Executive and Judicial officers of a State, or the members of the Legislature thereof, is denied to any of the male inhabitants of such State, being twenty-one years of age, and citizens of the United States, or in any way abridged, except for participation in rebellion, or other crime, the basis of representation therein shall be reduced in the

proportion which the number of such male citizens shall bear to the whole number of male citizens twenty-one years of age in such State.

3.   No person shall be a Senator or Representative in Congress, or elector of President and Vice-President, or hold any office, civil or military, under the United States, or under any State, who, having previously taken an oath, as a member of Congress, or as an officer of the United States, or as a member of any State legislature, or as an executive or judicial officer of any State, to support the Constitution of the United States, shall have engaged in insurrection or rebellion against the same, or given aid or comfort to the enemies thereof. But Congress may by a vote of two-thirds of each House, remove such disability.

4.   The validity of the public debt of the United States, authorized by law, including debts incurred for payment of pensions and bounties for services in suppressing insurrection or rebellion, shall not be questioned. But neither the United States nor any State shall assume or pay any debt or obligation incurred in aid of insurrection or rebellion against the United States, or any claim for the loss or emancipation of any slave; but all such debts, obligations and claims shall be held illegal and void.

5.   The Congress shall have power to enforce, by appropriate legislation, the provisions of this article.

Amendment 15—Race No Bar to Vote. Ratified 2/3/1870.

1.   The right of citizens of the United States to vote shall not be denied or abridged by the United States or by any State on account of race, color, or previous condition of servitude.

2.   The Congress shall have power to enforce this article by appropriate legislation.

Amendment 16—Status of Income Tax Clarified. Ratified 2/3/1913.

The Congress shall have power to lay and collect taxes on incomes, from whatever source derived, without apportionment among the several States, and without regard to any census or enumeration.

Amendment 17—Senators Elected by Popular Vote. Ratified 4/8/1913.

The Senate of the United States shall be composed of two Senators from each State, elected by the people thereof, for six years; and each Senator shall have one vote. The electors in each State shall have the qualifications requisite for electors of the most numerous branch of the State legislatures.

When vacancies happen in the representation of any State in the Senate, the executive authority of such State shall issue writs of election to fill such vacancies: Provided, That the legislature of any State may empower the executive thereof to make temporary appointments until the people fill the vacancies by election as the legislature may direct.

This amendment shall not be so construed as to affect the election or term of any Senator chosen before it becomes valid as part of the Constitution.

Amendment 18—Liquor Abolished. Ratified 1/16/1919. Repealed by Amendment 21, 12/5/1933.

1. After one year from the ratification of this article the manufacture, sale, or transportation of intoxicating liquors within, the importation thereof into, or the exportation thereof from the United States and all territory subject to the jurisdiction thereof for beverage purposes is hereby prohibited.

2. The Congress and the several States shall have concurrent power to enforce this article by appropriate legislation.

3. This article shall be inoperative unless it shall have been ratified as an amendment to the Constitution by the legislatures of the several States, as provided in the Constitution, within seven years from the date of the submission hereof to the States by the Congress.

Amendment 19—Women's Suffrage. Ratified 8/18/1920.

The right of citizens of the United States to vote shall not be denied or abridged by the United States or by any State on account of sex.

Congress shall have power to enforce this article by appropriate legislation.

Amendment 20—Presidential, Congressional Terms. Ratified 1/23/1933.

1. The terms of the President and Vice President shall end at noon on the 20th day of January, and the terms of Senators and Representatives at noon on the 3d day of January, of the years in which such terms would have ended if this article had not been ratified; and the terms of their successors shall then begin.

2. The Congress shall assemble at least once in every year, and such meeting shall begin at noon on the 3d day of January, unless they shall by law appoint a different day.

3. If, at the time fixed for the beginning of the term of the President, the President elect shall have died, the Vice President elect shall become President. If a President shall not have been chosen before the time fixed for the beginning of his term, or if the President elect shall have failed to qualify, then the Vice President elect shall act as President until a President shall have qualified; and the Congress may by law provide for the case wherein neither a President elect nor a Vice President elect shall have qualified, declaring who shall then act as President, or the manner in which one who is to act shall be selected, and such person shall act accordingly until a President or Vice President shall have qualified.

4. The Congress may by law provide for the case of the death of any of the persons from whom the House of Representatives may choose a President whenever the right of choice shall have devolved upon them, and for the case of the death of any of the persons from whom the Senate may choose a Vice President whenever the right of choice shall have devolved upon them.

5. Sections 1 and 2 shall take effect on the 15th day of October following the ratification of this article.

6. This article shall be inoperative unless it shall have been ratified as an amendment to the Constitution by the legislatures of three-fourths of the several States within seven years from the date of its submission.

Amendment 21—Amendment 18 Repealed. Ratified 12/5/1933.

1. The eighteenth article of amendment to the Constitution of the United States is hereby repealed.

2. The transportation or importation into any State, Territory, or possession of the United States for delivery or use therein of intoxicating liquors, in violation of the laws thereof, is hereby prohibited.

3. The article shall be inoperative unless it shall have been ratified as an amendment to the Constitution by conventions in the several States, as provided in the Constitution, within seven years from the date of the submission hereof to the States by the Congress.

Amendment 22—Presidential Term Limits. Ratified 2/27/1951.

1. No person shall be elected to the office of the President more than twice, and no person who has held the office of President, or acted as President, for more than two years of a term to which some other person was elected President shall be elected to the office of the President more than once. But this Article shall not apply to any person holding the office of President, when this Article was proposed by the Congress, and shall not prevent any person who may be holding the office of President, or acting as President, during the term within which this Article becomes operative from holding the office of President or acting as President during the remainder of such term.

2. This article shall be inoperative unless it shall have been ratified as an amendment to the Constitution by the legislatures of three-fourths of the several States within seven years from the date of its submission to the States by the Congress.

Amendment 23—Presidential Vote for District of Columbia. Ratified 3/29/1961.

1. The District constituting the seat of Government of the United States shall appoint in such manner as the Congress may direct: A number of electors of President and Vice President equal to the whole number of Senators and Representatives in Congress to which the District would be entitled if it were a State, but in no event more than the least populous State; they shall be in addition to those appointed by the States, but they shall be considered, for the purposes of the election of President and Vice President, to be electors

appointed by a State; and they shall meet in the District and perform such duties as provided by the twelfth article of amendment.

2. The Congress shall have power to enforce this article by appropriate legislation.

Amendment 24—Poll Tax Barred. Ratified 1/23/1964.

1. The right of citizens of the United States to vote in any primary or other election for President or Vice President, for electors for President or Vice President, or for Senator or Representative in Congress, shall not be denied or abridged by the United States or any State by reason of failure to pay any poll tax or other tax.

2. The Congress shall have power to enforce this article by appropriate legislation.

Amendment 25—Presidential Disability and Succession. Ratified 2/10/1967.

1. In case of the removal of the President from office or of his death or resignation, the Vice President shall become President.

2. Whenever there is a vacancy in the office of the Vice President, the President shall nominate a Vice President who shall take office upon confirmation by a majority vote of both Houses of Congress.

3. Whenever the President transmits to the President pro tempore of the Senate and the Speaker of the House of Representatives his written declaration that he is unable to discharge the powers and duties of his office, and until he transmits to them a written declaration to the contrary, such powers and duties shall be discharged by the Vice President as Acting President.

4. Whenever the Vice President and a majority of either the principal officers of the executive departments or of such other body as Congress may by law provide, transmit to the President pro tempore of the Senate and the Speaker of the House of Representatives their written declaration that the President is unable to discharge the powers and duties of his office, the Vice President shall immediately assume the powers and duties of the office as Acting President.

Thereafter, when the President transmits to the President pro tempore of the Senate and the Speaker of the House of Representatives his written declaration that no inability exists, he shall resume the powers and duties of his office unless the Vice President and a majority of either the principal officers of the executive department or of such other body as Congress may by law provide, transmit within four days to the President pro tempore of the Senate and the Speaker of the House of Representatives their written declaration that the President is unable to discharge the powers and duties of his office. Thereupon Congress shall decide the issue, assembling within forty eight hours for that purpose if not in session. If the Congress, within twenty one days after receipt of the latter written declaration, or, if Congress is not in session, within twenty one days after Congress is required to assemble, determines by two thirds vote of both Houses that the President is unable to discharge the powers and duties of his office, the Vice President shall continue to discharge the same as Acting President; otherwise, the President shall resume the powers and duties of his office.

Amendment 26—Voting Age Set to 18 Years. Ratified 7/1/1971.

1. The right of citizens of the United States, who are eighteen years of age or older, to vote shall not be denied or abridged by the United States or by any State on account of age.

2. The Congress shall have power to enforce this article by appropriate legislation.

Amendment 27—Limiting Congressional Pay Increases. Ratified 5/7/1992.

No law, varying the compensation for the services of the Senators and Representatives, shall take effect, until an election of Representatives shall have intervened.

Excerpt from Washington's Farewell Address

17th September 1796

Friends, And Fellow Citizens

The period for a new election of a citizen to administer the executive government of the United States, being not far distant, and the time actually arrived when your thoughts must be employed in designating the person who is to be clothed with that important trust, it appears to me proper, especially as it may conduce to a more distinct expression of the public voice, that I should now apprise you of the resolution I have formed, to decline being considered among the number of those out of whom a choice is to be made.

I beg you, at the same time, to do me the justice to be assured that this resolution has not been taken without a strict regard to all the considerations appertaining to the relation which binds a dutiful citizen to his country; and that, in withdrawing the tender of service which silence in my situation might imply, I am influenced by no diminution of zeal for your future interest; no deficiency of grateful respect for your past kindness; but am supported by a full conviction that the step is compatible with both....

I rejoice, that the state of your concerns, external as well as internal, no longer renders the pursuit of inclination incompatible with the sentiment of duty, or propriety; and am persuaded whatever partiality may be retained for my services, that, in the present circumstances of our country, you will not disapprove my determination to retire.

The impressions, with which, I first undertook the arduous trust, were explained on the proper occasion. In the discharge of this trust, I will only say that I have, with good intentions, contributed towards the organization and administration of the government the best exertions of which a very fallible judgment was capable.... I have the consolation to believe, that while choice and prudence invite me to quit the political scene, patriotism does not forbid it.

In looking forward to the moment, which is intended to terminate the career of my public life, my feelings do not permit me to suspend the deep acknowledgment of that debt of gratitude which I owe to my beloved country for the many honors it has conferred upon me; still more for the steadfast confidence with which it has supported me; and for the opportunities I have thence enjoyed of manifesting my inviolable attachment, by services faithful and persevering, though in usefulness unequal to my zeal....

Here, perhaps, I ought to stop. But a solicitude for your welfare which cannot end but with my life, and the apprehension of danger natural to that solicitude, urge me, on an occasion like the present, to offer to your solemn contemplation, and to recommend to your frequent review, some sentiments which are the result of much reflection, of no inconsiderable observation, and which appear to me all important to the permanency of your felicity as a people....

The unity of government which constitutes you one people, is also now dear to you. It is justly so: for it is a main pillar in the edifice of your real independence, the support of your tranquility at home, your peace abroad; of your safety; of your prosperity; of that very liberty which you so highly prize. But as it is easy to foresee that, from different causes and from different quarters, much pains will be taken, many artifices employed, to weaken in your minds the conviction of this truth; as this is the point in your political fortress against which the batteries of internal and external enemies will be most constantly and actively (though often covertly and insidiously) directed, it is of infinite moment that you should properly estimate the immense value of your national Union to your collective and individual happiness; that you should cherish a cordial, habitual, and immoveable attachment to it; accustoming yourself to think and speak of it as of the palladium of your political safety and prosperity; watching for its preservation with jealous anxiety; discountenancing whatever may suggest even a suspicion that it can in any event be abandoned; and indignantly frowning upon the first dawning of every attempt to alienate any portion of our country from the rest ...

For this you have every inducement of sympathy and interest. Citizens, by birth or choice, of a common country, that country has a right to concentrate your affections. The name of AMERICAN, which belongs to you in your national capacity, must always exalt the just pride of patriotism, more than any appellation derived from local discriminations....

In contemplating the causes which may disturb our Union, it occurs as matter of serious concern, that any ground should have been furnished for characterizing parties by geographical discriminations, Northern and Southern, Atlantic and Western; whence designing men may endeavor to excite a belief that there is a real difference of local interests and views. One of the expedients of party to acquire influence, within particular districts, is to misrepresent the opinions and aims of other districts. You cannot shield yourselves too much against the jealousies and heart burnings which spring from these misrepresentations; they tend to render alien to each other those who ought to be bound together by fraternal affection..... .

Sensible of this momentous truth, you have improved upon your first essay, by the adoption of a constitution of government better calculated than your former for an intimate union, and for the efficacious management of your common concerns. This government, the offspring of our own choice, uninfluenced and unawed, adopted upon full investigation and mature deliberation, completely free in its principles, in the distribution of its powers uniting security with energy, and containing within itself a provision for its own amendment, has a just claim to your confidence and your support. Respect for its authority, compliance with its laws, acquiescence in its measures, are duties enjoined by the fundamental maxims of true liberty. The basis of our political systems is the right of the people to make and to alter their constitutions of government. But the constitution which at any time exists, till changed by an explicit and authentic act of the whole people, is sacredly obligatory upon all. The very idea of the power and the right of the people to establish government presupposes the duty of every individual to obey the established government. All obstructions to the execution of the Laws, all combinations and associations, under whatever plausible character, with the real design to direct, control counteract, or awe the regular deliberation and action of the constituted authorities are destructive of this fundamental principle and of fatal tendency. They serve to organize faction, to give it an artificial and extraordinary force; to put, in the place of the delegated will of the nation, the will of a party, often a small but artful and enterprising minority of the community; and, according to the alternate triumphs of different parties, to make the public administration the mirror of the illconcerted and incongruous projects of faction, rather than the organ of consistent and wholesome plans digested by common councils, and modified by mutual interests.

However combinations or associations of the above description may now and then answer popular ends, they are likely, in the course of time and things, to become potent engines, by which cunning, ambitious and unprincipled men will be enabled to subvert the power of the people, and to usurp for themselves the reins of Government; destroying afterwards the very engines which have lifted them to unjust dominion....

I have already intimated to you the danger of parties in the state, with particular reference to the founding of them on geographical discriminations. Let me now take a more comprehensive view, and warn you in the most solemn manner against the baneful effects of the spirit of party, generally.

This spirit, unfortunately, is inseparable from our nature, having its root in the strongest passions of the human mind. It exists under different shapes in all governments, more or less stifled, controlled, or repressed; but in those of the popular form, it is seen in its greatest rankness, and is truly their worst enemy.

The alternate domination of one faction over another, sharpened by the spirit of revenge, natural to party dissention, which in different ages and countries has perpetrated the most horrid enormities, is itself a frightful despotism. But this leads at length to a more formal and permanent despotism....

Without looking forward to an extremity of this kind (which nevertheless ought not to be entirely out of sight), the common and continual mischiefs of the spirit of party are sufficient to make it the interest and duty of a wise people to discourage and restrain it.

It serves always to distract the public councils, and enfeeble the public administration. It agitates the community with ill founded jealousies and false alarms; kindles the animosity of one part against another, foments occasionally riot and insurrection. It opens the door to foreign influence and corruption, which find a facilitated access to the government itself through the channels of party passions....

There is an opinion, that parties in free countries are useful checks upon the administration of the government and serve to keep alive the spirit of liberty. This within certain limits is probably true; and in governments of a monarchical cast, patriotism may look with indulgence, if not with favor, upon the spirit of party. But in those of the popular character, in governments purely elective, it is a spirit not to be encouraged. From their natural tendency, it is certain there will always be enough of that spirit for every salutary purpose. And there being constant danger of excess, the effort ought to be, by force of public opinion, to mitigate and assuage it. A fire not to be quenched, it demands a uniform vigilance to prevent its bursting into a flame, lest, instead of warming, it should consume.

It is important, likewise, that the habits of thinking in a free country should inspire caution, in those entrusted with its administration, to confine themselves within their respective constitutional spheres, avoiding in the exercise of the powers of one department to encroach upon another. The spirit of encroachment tends to consolidate the powers of all the departments in one, and thus to create, whatever the form of government, a real despotism. A just estimate of that love of power, and proneness to abuse it, which predominates in the human heart, is sufficient to satisfy us of the truth of this position. The necessity of reciprocal checks in the exercise of political power, by dividing and distributing it into different depositories, and constituting each the guardian of the public weal against invasions by the others, has been evinced by experiments ancient and modern; some of them in our country and under our own eyes. To preserve them must be as necessary as to institute them....

In offering to you, my countrymen, these counsels of an old and affectionate friend, I dare not hope they will make the strong and lasting impression I could wish; that they will control the usual current of the passions, or prevent our nation from running the course which has hitherto marked the destiny of nations. But if I may even flatter myself that they may be productive of some partial benefit, some occasional good; that they may now and then recur to moderate the fury of party spirit, to warn against the mischiefs of foreign intrigue, to guard against the impostures of pretended patriotism; this hope will be a full recompense for the solicitude for your welfare by which they have been dictated.

How far in the discharge of my official duties I have been guided by the principles which have been delineated, the public records and other evidences of my conduct must witness to you and to the world. To myself, the assurance of my own conscience is, that I have at least believed myself to be guided by them....

Relying on its kindness in this as in other things, and actuated by that fervent love towards it which is so natural to a man who views in it the native soil of himself and his progenitors for several generations, I anticipate with pleasing expectation that retreat in which I promise myself to realize, without alloy, the sweet enjoyment of partaking, in the midst of my fellow citizens, the benign influence of good laws under a free government, the ever favorite object of my heart, and the happy reward, as I trust, of our mutual cares, labors and dangers.

George Washington

Kennedy Inaugural Address

✦

January 20, 1961

Vice President Johnson, Mr. Speaker, Mr. Chief Justice, President Eisenhower, Vice President Nixon, President Truman, reverend clergy, fellow citizens, we observe today not a victory of party, but a celebration of freedom—symbolizing an end, as well as a beginning—signifying renewal, as well as change. For I have sworn before you and Almighty God the same solemn oath our forebears prescribed nearly a century and three quarters ago.

The world is very different now. For man holds in his mortal hands the power to abolish all forms of human poverty and all forms of human life. And yet the same revolutionary beliefs for which our forebears fought are still at issue around the globe—the belief that the rights of man come not from the generosity of the state, but from the hand of God.

We dare not forget today that we are the heirs of that first revolution. Let the word go forth from this time and place, to friend and foe alike, that the torch has been passed to a new generation of Americans—born in this century, tempered by war, disciplined by a hard and bitter peace, proud of our ancient heritage—and unwilling to witness or permit the slow undoing of those human rights to which this Nation has always been committed, and to which we are committed today at home and around the world.

Let every nation know, whether it wishes us well or ill, that we shall pay any price, bear any burden, meet any hardship, support any friend, oppose any foe, in order to assure the survival and the success of liberty.

This much we pledge—and more.

To those old allies whose cultural and spiritual origins we share, we pledge the loyalty of faithful friends. United, there is little we cannot do in a host of cooperative ventures. Divided, there is little we can do—for we dare not meet a powerful challenge at odds and split asunder.

To those new States whom we welcome to the ranks of the free, we pledge our word that one form of colonial control shall not have passed away merely to be replaced by a far more iron tyranny. We shall not always expect to find them supporting our view. But we shall always hope to find them strongly supporting their own freedom—and to remember that, in the past, those who foolishly sought power by riding the back of the tiger ended up inside.

To those peoples in the huts and villages across the globe struggling to break the bonds of mass misery, we pledge our best efforts to help them help themselves, for whatever period is required—not because the Communists may be doing it, not because we seek their votes, but because it is right. If a free society cannot help the many who are poor, it cannot save the few who are rich.

To our sister republics south of our border, we offer a special pledge—to convert our good words into good deeds—in a new alliance for progress—to assist free men and free governments in casting off the chains of poverty. But this peaceful revolution of hope cannot become the prey of hostile powers. Let all our neighbors know that we shall join with them to oppose aggression or subversion anywhere in the Americas. And let every other power know that this Hemisphere intends to remain the master of its own house.

To that world assembly of sovereign states, the United Nations, our last best hope in an age where the instruments of war have far outpaced the instruments of peace, we renew our pledge of support—to prevent it from becoming merely a forum for invective—to strengthen its shield of the new and the weak—and to enlarge the area in which its writ may run.

Finally, to those nations who would make themselves our adversary, we offer not a pledge but a request: that both sides begin anew the quest for peace, before the dark powers of destruction unleashed by science engulf all humanity in planned or accidental self-destruction

We dare not tempt them with weakness. For only when our arms are sufficient beyond doubt can we be certain beyond doubt that they will never be employed. But neither can two great and powerful groups of nations take comfort from our present course—both sides overburdened by the cost of modern weapons, both rightly alarmed by the steady spread of the deadly atom, yet both racing to alter that uncertain balance of terror that stays the hand of mankind's final war.

So let us begin anew—remembering on both sides that civility is not a sign of weakness, and sincerity is always subject to proof. Let us never negotiate out of fear. But let us never fear to negotiate.

Let both sides explore what problems unite us instead of belaboring those problems which divide us.

Let both sides, for the first time, formulate serious and precise proposals for the inspection and control of arms—and bring the absolute power to destroy other nations under the absolute control of all nations.

Let both sides seek to invoke the wonders of science instead of its terrors. Together let us explore the stars, conquer the deserts, eradicate disease, tap the ocean depths, and encourage the arts and commerce

Let both sides unite to heed in all corners of the earth the command of Isaiah—to "undo the heavy burdens ... and to let the oppressed go free."

And if a beachhead of cooperation may push back the jungle of suspicion, let both sides join in creating a new endeavor, not a new balance of power, but a new world of law, where the strong are just and the weak secure and the peace preserved.

All this will not be finished in the first 100 days. Nor will it be finished in the first 1,000 days, nor in the life of this Administration, nor even perhaps in our lifetime on this planet. But let us begin.

In your hands, my fellow citizens, more than in mine, will rest the final success or failure of our course. Since this country was founded, each generation of Americans has been summoned to give testimony to its national loyalty. The graves of young Americans who answered the call to service surround the globe.

Now the trumpet summons us again—not as a call to bear arms, though arms we need; not as a call to battle, though embattled we are—but a call to bear the burden of a long twilight struggle, year in and year out, "rejoicing in hope, patient in tribulation"—a struggle against the common enemies of man: tyranny, poverty, disease, and war itself

Can we forge against these enemies a grand and global alliance, North and South, East and West, that can assure a more fruitful life for all mankind? Will you join in that historic effort?

In the long history of the world, only a few generations have been granted the role of defending freedom in its hour of maximum danger. I do not shrink from this responsibility—I welcome it. I do not believe that any of us would exchange places with any other people or any other generation. The energy, the faith, the devotion which we bring to this endeavor will light our country and all who serve it—and the glow from that fire can truly light the world.

And so, my fellow Americans: ask not what your country can do for you—ask what you can do for your country.

My fellow citizens of the world: ask not what America will do for you, but what together we can do for the freedom of man.

Finally, whether you are citizens of America or citizens of the world, ask of us the same high standards of strength and sacrifice which we ask of you. With a good conscience our only sure reward, with history the final judge of our deeds, let us go forth to lead the land we love, asking His blessing and His help, but knowing that here on earth God's work must truly be our own.

Excerpts from Kennedy Speech on Space Exploration

♦

May 25, 1961

IX. SPACE

Finally, if we are to win the battle that is now going on around the world between freedom and tyranny, the dramatic achievements in space which occurred in recent weeks should have made clear to us all, as did the Sputnik in 1957, the impact of this adventure on the minds of men everywhere, who are attempting to make a determination of which road they should take..... [W]e have examined where we are strong and where we are not, where we may succeed and where we may not. Now it is time to take longer strides—time for a great new American enterprise—time for this nation to take a clearly leading role in space achievement, which in many ways may hold the key to our future on earth. I believe we possess all the resources and talents necessary. But the facts of the matter are that we have never made the national decisions or marshalled the national resources required for such leadership. We have never specified long-range goals on an urgent time schedule, or managed our resources and our time so as to insure their fulfillment.....

First, I believe that this nation should commit itself to achieving the goal, before this decade is out, of landing a man on the moon and returning him safely to the earth.....

Let it be clear—and this is a judgment which the Members of the Congress must finally make—let it be clear that I am asking the Congress and the country to accept a firm commitment to a new course of action, a course which will last for many years and carry very heavy costs:....

[B]ecause it is a heavy burden, and there is no sense in agreeing or desiring that the United States take an affirmative position in outer space, unless we are prepared to do the work and bear the burdens to make it successful. If we are not, we should decide today and this year.

This decision demands a major national commitment of scientific and technical manpower, materiel and facilities, and the possibility of their diversion from other important activities where they are already thinly spread. It means a degree of dedication, organization and discipline which have not always characterized our research and development efforts. It means we cannot afford undue work stoppages, inflated costs of material or talent, wasteful interagency rivalries, or a high turnover of key personnel.

New objectives and new money cannot solve these problems. They could in fact, aggravate them further—unless every scientist, every engineer, every serviceman, every technician, contractor, and civil servant gives his personal pledge that this nation will move forward, with the full speed of freedom, in the exciting adventure of space.

Excerpt from Martin Luther King-I Have a Dream Speech

◆

August 28, 1963

I am happy to join with you today in what will go down in history as the greatest demonstration for freedom in the history of our nation.

Five score years ago, a great American, in whose symbolic shadow we stand today, signed the Emancipation Proclamation. This momentous decree came as a great beacon light of hope to millions of Negro slaves who had been seared in the flames of withering injustice. It came as a joyous daybreak to end the long night of their captivity.

But one hundred years later, the Negro still is not free. One hundred years later, the life of the Negro is still sadly crippled by the manacles of segregation and the chains of discrimination. One hundred years later, the Negro lives on a lonely island of poverty in the midst of a vast ocean of material prosperity. One hundred years later, the Negro is still languishing in the corners of American society and finds himself an exile in his own land. So we have come here today to dramatize a shameful condition....

This is no time to engage in the luxury of cooling off or to take the tranquilizing drug of gradualism. Now is the time to make real the promises of democracy. Now is the time to rise from the dark and desolate valley of segregation to the sunlit path of racial justice. Now is the time to lift our nation from the quick sands of racial injustice to the solid rock of brotherhood. Now is the time to make justice a reality for all of God's children....

But there is something that I must say to my people who stand on the warm threshold which leads into the palace of justice. In the process of gaining our rightful place we must not be guilty of wrongful deeds. Let us not seek to satisfy our thirst for freedom by drinking from the cup of bitterness and hatred.

We must forever conduct our struggle on the high plane of dignity and discipline. We must not allow our creative protest to degenerate into physical violence. Again and again we must rise to the majestic heights of meeting physical force with soul force. The marvelous new militancy which has engulfed the Negro community must not lead us to a distrust of all white people, for many of our white brothers, as evidenced by their presence here today, have come to realize that their destiny is tied up with our destiny. They have come to realize that their freedom is inextricably bound to our freedom. We cannot walk alone.

As we walk, we must make the pledge that we shall always march ahead. We cannot turn back. There are those who are asking the devotees of civil rights, "When will you be satisfied?" We can never be satisfied as long as the Negro is the victim of the unspeakable horrors of police brutality. We can never be satisfied, as long as our bodies, heavy with the fatigue of travel, cannot gain lodging in the motels of the highways and the hotels of the cities. We cannot be satisfied as long as the Negro's basic mobility is from a smaller ghetto to a larger one. We can never be satisfied as long as our children are stripped of their selfhood and robbed of their dignity by signs stating "For Whites Only". We cannot be satisfied as long as a Negro in Mississippi cannot vote and a Negro in New York believes he has nothing for which to vote. No, no, we are not satisfied, and we will not be satisfied until justice rolls down like waters and righteousness like a mighty stream.

I am not unmindful that some of you have come here out of great trials and tribulations. Some of you have come fresh from narrow jail cells. Some of you have come from areas where your quest for freedom left you battered by the storms of persecution and staggered by the winds of police brutality. You have been the veterans of creative suffering. Continue to work with the faith that unearned suffering is redemptive.

Go back to Mississippi, go back to Alabama, go back to South Carolina, go back to Georgia, go back to Louisiana, go back to the slums and ghettos of our northern cities, knowing that somehow this situation can and will be changed. Let us not wallow in the valley of despair.

I say to you today, my friends, so even though we face the difficulties of today and tomorrow, I still have a dream. It is a dream deeply rooted in the American dream.

I have a dream that one day this nation will rise up and live out the true meaning of its creed: "We hold these truths to be self-evident: that all men are created equal."

I have a dream that one day on the red hills of Georgia the sons of former slaves and the sons of former slave owners will be able to sit down together at the table of brotherhood.

I have a dream that one day even the state of Mississippi, a state sweltering with the heat of injustice, sweltering with the heat of oppression, will be transformed into an oasis of freedom and justice.

I have a dream that my four little children will one day live in a nation where they will not be judged by the color of their skin but by the content of their character.

I have a dream today.

I have a dream that one day, down in Alabama, with its vicious racists, with its governor having his lips dripping with the words of interposition and nullification; one day right there in Alabama, little black boys and black girls will be able to join hands with little white boys and white girls as sisters and brothers.

I have a dream today.

I have a dream that one day every valley shall be exalted, every hill and mountain shall be made low, the rough places will be made plain, and the crooked places will be made straight, and the glory of the Lord shall be revealed, and all flesh shall see it together.

This is our hope. This is the faith that I go back to the South with. With this faith we will be able to hew out of the mountain of despair a stone of hope. With this faith we will be able to transform the jangling discords of our nation into a beautiful symphony of brotherhood. With this faith we will be able to work together, to pray together, to struggle together, to go to jail together, to stand up for freedom together, knowing that we will be free one day.

This will be the day when all of God's children will be able to sing with a new meaning, "My country, 'tis of thee, sweet land of liberty, of thee I sing. Land where my fathers died, land of the pilgrim's pride, from every mountainside, let freedom ring."

And if America is to be a great nation this must become true. So let freedom ring from the prodigious hilltops of New Hampshire. Let freedom ring from the mighty mountains of New York. Let freedom ring from the heightening Alleghenies of Pennsylvania!

Let freedom ring from the snowcapped Rockies of Colorado!

Let freedom ring from the curvaceous slopes of California!

But not only that; let freedom ring from Stone Mountain of Georgia!

Let freedom ring from Lookout Mountain of Tennessee!

Let freedom ring from every hill and molehill of Mississippi. From every mountainside, let freedom ring.

And when this happens, when we allow freedom to ring, when we let it ring from every village and every hamlet, from every state and every city, we will be able to speed up that day when all of God's children, black men and white men, Jews and Gentiles, Protestants and Catholics, will be able to join hands and sing in the words of the old Negro spiritual, "Free at last! free at last! thank God Almighty, we are free at last!"

978-0-595-51789-3
0-595-51789-7